EL GRA   DER

Please return / renew by date shown.
You can renew it at:
norlink.norfolk.gov.uk
or by telephone: 0344 800 8006
Please have your library card & PIN ready

NORFOLK LIBRARY
AND INFORMATION SERVICE

Nothing More to Lose

Being a hero isn't worth the effort – or so Buck Buckley reckons. And he ought to know. The day he foils the Green River bank robbery is the day he becomes a Hero with a capital 'H'. The attention that follows is the last thing Buckley wants or needs.

Locals can't understand Buckley's resistance, but they do not know the secrets he is hiding. Buckley is desperate to disappear again and return to being a nobody. But a picture appears in the papers and his past begins to catch up with him. As his new-found fame puts him in the firing line, he must stop running and address his demons face on in a final showdown.

By the same author

A Land to Die For
Deathwatch Trail
Buckskin Girl
Longshot
Vigilante Marshal
Five Graves West
The Brazos Legacy
Big Bad River
Reno's Renegades
Red Sunday
Wrong Side of the River
Longhorn Country
Cheyenne Gallows
Dead Where You Stand!
Durango Gunhawk
Knife Edge
Wilde Country
Rawhide Ransom
Brazos Fugitive
Dead-End Trail
Cut-Price Lawman
Rogue's Run
Fargo's Legacy
Mr Gunn
Dead Man River

Nothing More to Lose

Tyler Hatch

A Black Horse Western

ROBERT HALE · LONDON

© Tyler Hatch 2015
First published in Great Britain 2015

ISBN 978-0-7198-1760-1

Robert Hale Limited
Clerkenwell House
Clerkenwell Green
London EC1R 0HT

www.halebooks.com

Printed and bound in Great Britain by
CPI Antony Rowe, Chippenham and Eastbourne

CHAPTER 1

HERO

It had been a long, hot ride into town from the valley and if he hadn't stopped in the saloon for a drink on his way to the livery, the man calling himself 'Buck' Buckley wouldn't have run into Herb Barry in the bar – and learned that Herb was quitting Grantland Town. For keeps.

'Comes as a bit of a—no, a *big* surprise, Herb. Sudden-like, ain't it?' he asked as he settled at the bar, an easy-moving man somewhere in his mid thirties. Barry, now alongside him, was a weary-looking middle-aged cowman with a drooping moustache and a weathered face.

Herb sniffed through his prominent nose and nodded, lifting rheumy blue eyes to the taller Buckley's face. 'Most of the wife's family got wiped out in that big fire up in Carlton Creek – couple of the kids were away an' survived, and, well, you know women: she's just gotta go and take care of 'em.'

'Seems the thing to do, Herb,' Buckley said quietly.

'Yeah, yeah, I know. Aw, they're good kids and I got no real beef about helpin' 'em out, but – well, hell, I just signed up for the last ten acres of Lee Barnes's old spread! The bank's handlin' things, of course, now that Lee's moved out. You know the parcel I mean?'

'Yeah. But, you paid what he was askin'?' Buckley blinked, surprised. 'He was reaching for the sky, you know!'

Herb threw him a crooked grin. 'Beat him down, would you believe! *Me*, beatin' that old skinflint down to only a few hundred more'n I really wanted to pay!' He shook his head jerkily. 'Can't believe I done it. Now, I ain't even gonna get a chance to *use* the land. Once Hattie gets up there with them boys, she won't wanna come back here … have to sell up, lock, stock and both damn barrels!'

'Mighty tough luck, Herb. I had my eye on that land myself, one time, but couldn't come anywhere near what Lee was askin' for it … still couldn't, for the matter of that.'

Herb suddenly looked a lot more interested. 'Hey! Buck, ol' *amigo*, I got me an idea…. See, I'm in a bit of a bind: I *can* get the money, but it has to be a bank loan.'

'You talked Banker Farnham into a loan?' Buckley couldn't hide his genuine surprise this time. '*Nice work!*'

Herb shrugged. 'Yeah. Don't ask me how, but he

agreed. Thing is, now I have to take it, paper's all signed, and so on, see? Gotta pay the damn thing off, but it'll be down here while I'm all the way up in Carlton Crick! I explained about the wife's kin and he seemed like he was truly sympathetic, but said he can't change the bank's rules.'

'Well, you know how banks always cover their asses no matter what.'

Herb nodded, his mouth pulled down into a bitter curve. 'Only other way is for me to find someone else to take over the loan....'

He let the words trail off and there was more than a hint in his arched eyebrows. 'What do you think, Buck?'

'Aw, now, wait up! I'd have to think damn *hard* about that!'

Yeah, sure, Buck. I know it's kinda miserable sluggin' you like this, an' I'm sorry, pard, but I just ain't got a lotta time.'

'I'm sorry, too, Herb, 'cause I ain't got a lotta *money*! Nowhere close to what I'd need for a deposit and—'

Herb grabbed Buck's right arm and immediately jumped back when the man slapped it away – hard.

'Judas Priest, Buck! You damn near broke my hand!' Herb rubbed briskly at his numbing hand and fingers.

'Didn't mean to slap so hard, Herb, but I— just don't like anyone grappling with my gun arm. Never have.'

'*Gun arm*! I never heard you was touchy about a thing like *that*! You talkin' about your *gun* arm! Cheez!'

Buck looked uncomfortable. 'Let's call it an old habit – dies hard, and leave it at that. But, Herb, you really think if I went and saw the banker…?'

'Good chance he'd transfer the loan, but, Buck, you'd have to put up your entire spread, literally, everything you own as … aaah! I forget what you call it—'

' "Collateral." I savvy that, Herb. I've had bank loans before. Long time back. Had me a wife then, too, and another na—' He cut the last word off like a falling axe.

'Hell! You're full of surprises today, Buck.' Herb looked up quickly as the town clock rang out the noon bell. 'Dammit! I'm runnin' late, and the wife … well, you know Hattie. Listen, go see Farnham an' I'll get round there soon as I can, and, with any luck, between us … OK?'

He winked and Buck nodded abruptly, having made his decision. 'Right! I'll give it a go.' *He'd be loco to pass up a chance like this!*

Herb was already moving away – briskly now – and Buck Buckley left the bar and found some shade under the old-style saloon's veranda roof while he rolled a cigarette and smoked it down slowly, thinking of the step he was about to take.

It would be a might big one for him. He didn't like being locked into loans, whether they were from a bank or an individual, but, with that land, he could go into the Gauntlet Hills, round up enough mavericks to swell his small herd, and that would give him extra money, so that, come sale time, he could maybe even pay off the loan sooner.

'Hell, man!' he said, half aloud. 'You're way ahead of yourself! Go see the banker first ... take it from there.'

So he flicked away the butt of the cigarette, hitched up his trousers and gunbelt, then crossed the street to the Green River First National Bank. He paused briefly with his hand on the handle of the closed door. *Closed? Not like Banker Farnham to risk missing a customer. Ah!* It wasn't locked as he'd thought. The tongue of the lock must've just caught up in the socket edge, that was all. The door swung inwards—

And Buck Buckley stepped into a whole slew of 'fame' he neither wanted, and sure as hell didn't need....

Two steps inside, the door swinging closed behind him, Buck stopped. There was a group of people gathered at the end of the main counter, huddled together and looking mighty anxious, some openly scared, obviously of another group who had drawn guns covering them!

All eyes turned to him as he entered and one of the men with a gun in each hand swore. 'Thought I tell you to lack that verdammed door, din' I, Loop!' he growled.

'Thought I did, Jack,' said one of the others, voice a mite shaky: a young man with a worried, broad face, almost moon-like. 'The – the lock was kinda stiff, though.'

The big man ignored him and swung his six-gun

towards Buckley who had paused in mid-stride now. He'd recognized the big man with the accent as German Jack, an outlaw who had been on the run for months after a bank robbery at Broken Fork in the neighbouring county – a man who was known for not leaving any witnesses to his deeds.

Jack raised his voice now, his gun covering Buckley. 'Come join the party, *mein Bekannter* – Ve are all friends here – for the moment! Ve mebbe help you with your money, eh? How much you like to giff me…?'

Buckley replied quietly, 'I don't have enough to give any away.'

'Aaah! Anudder poor man, eh!' German Jack spat on the floor. 'Dis town is full of dem! But ve vill manage. Tell me how much you vant an' I giff it to you – nice and friendly, eh?'

'Yeah, that's friendly. But I like to do my own banking business, thanks all the same.'

German Jack waved his pistol that was like a toy in his big hand, and laughed – a great booming sound that caught the attention of the robbers: they all grinned, including the worried-looking youngster with the moon face.

'Hey, comrades! You hear dat! Very polite, dis fellow, but I t'ink ve help him anyvay! Turn out your pockets, eh?'

'They're empty – that's why I came in here – to get some money to put in 'em.'

'Aw! I t'ink you getting smart vit' me, now!' Jack lifted his left hand and moved his thick index finger slowly back and forth. 'Not nice! So, ve vaste no more time on you!'

'No use running, Jack, everyone knows who you are,' Buckley told him quietly.

'Dat's good! An' they vill know who *you* are! It vill be on your tombstone: *"He knew the great German Jack!"* Pretty damn goot, eh?' The huge fist holding his gun began to rise. 'So, I make for *you* a deposit – *in lead*!'

His gun swung toward Buckley, the hammer spur firmly under the ball of his thumb. His teeth bared in sadistic humour as he bagan to lift that thumb ... just as the young robber with the round face said, 'Hey, Jack! I think I know this *hombre*. He's—'

Those who were there later tried to describe exactly what happened next, but it was just so damn fast that no two descriptions were the same.

Buckley, ignoring the young outlaw, crouched swiftly, shoulders and upper arms moving confidently and mighty fast ... *mighty fast*!

Fanning a six-gun is usually spectacular, always noisy, but mostly inaccurate ... unless the gun is shooting into a confined space.

And the corner of the bank where German Jack and his gang stood menacing the cowering customers and staff was mighty crowded, the robbers standing back in their own tight group a few feet from the others.

Unlucky for them!

Buckley's right hand blurred as he fanned the hammer spur. The shots were so close together they sounded like the shocking, prolonged roar of a Gatling gun at full speed. Flashes stabbed like fiery blades through the pall of billowing, choking smoke.

Seconds later, when that smoke began to lift, German Jack and his men could be seen writhing on the floor in a welter of blood, one man still falling to join the jumbled pile of his companions, jerking in the last moments of their lives.

'*Christ Almighty!*' someone said in an awed whisper. 'He – he's killed 'em all! One bullet each!'

There were screams, both male and female, a couple of the robbers' guns firing into the floor as trigger fingers jerked convulsively. A couple of windows shattered. People shouted and rushed in all directions, jamming the doorways.

'Stop panicking!' roared Buckley and, surprisingly, the crowd did. '*There's nothing to fear now!*'

He was already shucking smoking, used cartridges from his Colt's cylinder, calmly reloading, carefully checking his handiwork. 'Cool as a clam,' someone said later.

Then he looked at the huddled group, figured the bank staff members must be amongst them somewhere and said, 'One of you bank Johnnies get your window open, will you? I'm in a hurry to make my withdrawal.'

A white-faced clerk was opening his cage as well as he could with shaking hands and stammered, 'It – it will be an honour and a privilege to serve you, sir! I – I've never seen such – such gun-speed!'

The words were echoed by other staffers and shaky, but relieved, customers as they began to crowd round

Buckley now.

'Hey! Dammit! Gimme room!' he yelled. 'I said I'm in a hurry!'

He didn't need to wave his gun – the crowd cleared a space around the teller's window in a couple of fast breaths.

A man whom Buckley recognized as the sweating Manager – Farnham – stepped forward tentatively. 'Friend, you are not leaving here without at least my handshake, and any reward for the demise of German Jack, of course. You're a hero, man! And what a hero at that! You'll be famous throughout the entire South-West!'

Buckley's face tightened. *Why the hell couldn't he have minded his own business?* Immediately the thought came into his head, he knew, of course, that that hadn't been an option, but now – *now, Goddammit!*

It was too late!

Fame, glory, and reward – these were the things that Farnham was going on about.

And Buckley didn't want any part of them! Oh, sure, the money would be welcome, but – not now! Not this way with all the publicity that would follow.

Hell, his whole world had just blown up in his face.

'Mr Buckley, isn't it?' continued the bank manager eagerly. 'I believe I know your place, way out there in the Gauntlet Valley. Well, if ever you need help, financially, or in any other way, this bank is at your service.'

Farnham, never a man to miss an opportunity to boost his own image in the community, looked around, beaming and didn't seem to notice all the jaws dropping in surprise at his statement. Old Tight-Fist himself! Being *generous*! Some even glanced out the windows to make sure the sky wasn't falling in.

Then another citizen said, 'The whole damn town's yours, *amigo*! Ain't that so, friends...?'

And there were many voices avowing that.

'Hell! Make it the whole damn county!' a man shouted.

'Er, that's all very fine,' Buckley said, stopped to clear his voice, then added, 'I thank you. But, like I said, I'm in something of a hurry, so if I could have a few words with you in private, Mr Manager...?'

'Of course, sir! Of course. Come this way to my office. Oh, Mr Jackson, will you and your clerks attend to matters here while I...?' He gestured towards Buckley and the clerk he had spoken to puffed out his chest at being named in person – by The Manager! – and immediately began fussing over arrangements to cover the dead men just as a newcomer, sweating and gasping for breath, came staggering in through the side door, awkwardly, because of the cumbersome press camera he was trying to juggle.

'Gents! Gents!' he gasped. 'Please don't move! The next edition of our *Gazette* will be going to press within the hour. Please! Allow me to get your pictures, I beg you! This is a – a – momentous day for our town. Especially for you, sir. Our new hero! Your picture will take up at least half the front page, showing you to the world as you deserve! Now, could you please move over this way so I can get the light coming through the window? Oh, now, don't be modest! Ah, here's the Sheriff – at last! I see I don't have to urge *you* to get in the picture, Sheriff!'

'Just make damn sure there's room for me on that front page of your rag, too!' growled the big, hard-faced lawman who shouldered folk aside roughly, intent on hogging as big a slice of the limelight as possible.

He even winked as he took the rigid Buckley by the arm – the *left* one – and dragged him reluctantly into the slanting shaft of sunlight as the photographer set up his camera. Some of the folk who had been cornered by the robbers jostled for a better view and, hopefully, room enough to edge into the picture too.

But Buckley found himself in the fore with the now-grinning lawman beside him. 'Stand right along-side me, feller. You an' me've got some jawin' to do after this, by the way, reward money and so on....'

Buckley blinked involuntarily as he heard the clunk of the camera's shutter.

The cameraman sounded a mite exasperated as he said, 'Oh! Do try and smile a little, Mr Buckley! Please!'

He tried.

But he felt more like screaming.

CHAPTER 2

'HOWDY! YOU S.O.B.'

'It's him! Judas Priest, Murph! It is – *him!*'

The man lounging in a straightback chair, his boots up on a similar chair, only turned his head slightly as he yawned and looked at the man who had spoken.

'The hell you gettin' all excited about, Rainey? I'm too damned tired to get excited about anythin' right now.' He mixed up his next yawn with a snorted half-laugh. 'Man, I tell you that Brandy is well named! She sure packs a kick, but in all the right places!'

Rainey shook out the crumpled copy of the *Grantland Gazette* he was holding and turned it so the exhausted Murph could see the front page, half of which was taken up by a grainy picture of a startled-looking man beneath the words in large block capitals: *OUR HERO!*

'Look at this, dammit, an' forget that whore for a few minutes!' As Murph turned a mite more quickly now,

16

his face tight, Rainey added, 'It's him – Craddock!'

Murph froze his movement, flicked agate eyes to Rainey's face, a puzzled frown creasing his brow.

'Craddock...?' Murph actually hitched fully around in his chair now. 'Wayne Craddock? What in hell're you—?'

'Look at the damn picture, will you!' Rainey growled, shaking the paper now. 'Calls himself Buckley, but Hell! *Look*, for Chrissakes! No mistakin' him!'

Murph looked, his frown more pronounced as he lifted a hard stare in Rainey's direction. 'You goin' blind or something'? Hell, that's nothin' like Craddock: no moustache, sideburns – his hair's darker, shorter.'

'Christ! Look at the nose!' Rainey almost shouted and it made Murph jump.

'Nose? What? Aw, hell!'

'Yeah! At last! See the bridge with the two bumps, and that small, deep scar right back between his eyes, where it joins his head? I done that to him when we had that go-round in Laredo. It was about the only good punch I managed to land. He beat the crap outa me but he had to get outa town in a hurry, blood all over him – the nose was never set proper, an' – I'd bet my life it is him, Murph. It *is*!'

The intensity of Rainey's words pulled up Murph and he turned the paper this way and that, moving it into the weak sunlight coming through the smeared window, onto the features. As he procrastinated, Rainey said flatly, 'Murph, that picture ain't gonna change no matter how long you look at it. It … is … Wayne Craddock!'

'He musta shaved off the beard and so on …'

' 'Course he did! But I knew him long before he grew it for a disguise. That's why I'm sure it's Craddock.'

Murph's lips had been moving as he slowly read the accompanying copy in and around the picture. He lifted his gaze to Rainey's taut face.

'Well! If it is him—' He shook the paper briefly. 'An' – Godammit! I think it *is*! – well, "howdy-howdy", you son of a bitch. An' don't think you'll ride away this time.' He shook his head. 'You believe this? Says here he walked into the Green River National Bank in Grantland, smack in the middle of a hold-up by German Jack Schultz an' his gang. Shot 'em all to hell in about five seconds! Guess that's the hee-ro part.'

Rainey pursed his lips. 'Still a hotshot with a Colt then, ain't he? Fact he sounds deadlier than ever.'

Murph nodded a mite absently. 'Son of a bitch has been livin' less than a hundred miles from us all this time! What? Must be four, five years now, since—'

'About four and a half, Murph. Lotta water gone under the bridge.'

Murph's thick lips moved slightly – it may have been just the beginning of a smile. 'Says he has a ranch just off the trail to them Gauntlet Hills, sou'-west of Grantland. *Quiet-spoken, well liked rancher.* Well he ain't all *that* well liked, I'm here to tell you! Fact, I'll go on record an' say that Mr Pop-u-lar Hee-ro Craddock has

18

just about reached the end of his trail!'

Rainey nodded solemnly. 'A-men to that!'

.

The man who called himself Buck Buckley had come to more or less the same conclusion: he had to quit the trail he had been following for some years now, reluctantly!

But now he had been discovered, it was the only way to go – clear out and start anew.

And how many times had he done that already? Four? Five?

'Damned if I feel like doin' that! Damned if I do!'

He swore and crumpled his copy of the newspaper.

He should have grabbed that camera and busted it over the photographer's head! But then the sheriff would've started wondering why he didn't want his picture taken and demanded an explanation.

'Getting' soft, I reckon!' he muttered, referring to himself, and hurled the crumpled paper into the low-burning fire in the small fireplace of the dingy hotel room he was renting overnight before returning to Gauntlet Valley.

He watched with a sort of strange detachment, his own image distort and rapidly take on half-a-dozen different forms before bursting into flames and crumbling into a handful of ashes …

So, that was that!

'But too damn late, you fool!' he berated himself coldly. That picture would have been seen by hundreds of people by now and, although he had changed his appearance as much as he could, he knew there were plenty of men who might still recognize him even without all the old facial hair he'd been forced to wear after the last time his true identity had been discovered.

Yeah! It was time to go, all right. The word had spread fast throughout the south-west about his foiling the bank robbery; newspapers from all over would have paid for rights to use the story, spreading it far and wide; just what the public loved to read about – a quiet, pleasant-enough small rancher, minding his own business, and suddenly boosted into the limelight just by walking into that bank and tangling with German Jack and his band of robbers.

He had reacted as he had been trained to do: assessed the situation in a flash, knew intuitively that German Jack and his men wouldn't allow him to leave the bank alive, and then – the inevitable action....

Jack and his men bringing up their guns automatically just as he automatically responded with the old deadly instincts cutting in ... something he was powerless to prevent ... *drop to one knee for stability, angle the barrel, then—*

His left hand had blurred over the spur of the cocked hammer of his six-gun for just a few brief seconds with the deadly expertise and speed he had developed over the years. The Colt was fully loaded and in just under six seconds its lead was raking the startled bunch of robbers, cutting them down, fatally, one after the other.

Before they had hit the floor in a tangled bloody mess of limbs and quivering bodies, he was reloading.

Old habits die hard.

That was the truth of it: the old, murderous habits had jumped to the fore after all this time lying dormant. He ought to have known there was no escaping such a moment. It had had to happen! And now it had.

He could probably have lived with that, but that damn newspaper picture had compounded the whole blamed issue, by showing his face! He had known the moment he had seen it he would be might lucky if he escaped the natural consequences of such a happening!

Recognition was almost certainly inevitable, and then...? No prizes for guessing the answer to that!

He stared into the glowing coals; only a few unrecognizable ashes now, but that was only one copy of the damned rag of a newspaper.

How many more eyes had already seen his picture, and how many might have recognized him despite his efforts at disguise? Too damn many, he thought bitterly. And one thing was for sure, he was going to find out pretty soon – and the hard way!

Everybody wanted to shake his hand, the hand that had put paid to a bunch of outlaws who had run wild through this neck of the woods for three long years of terror.

It was a marathon, just walking down the streets

of Grantland, and he took to ducking into stores for goods by the freight entrance, loading the gear onto his packhorse before slipping out of town, hopefully unnoticed.

He didn't have much success at that, but cut his trips to town to a minimum and pulled every trick he knew to dodge pursuers – even those with good intentions like the citizens of Grantland – and get back to work on the many chores he had waiting for him at his spread in the Gauntlet Hills surrounding the valley of the same name.

He felt he had already sunk his roots too far down here in these hills to just pull up stakes and vamoose.

Maybe it would come to that in the end, but he decided, stubbornly, that he wasn't going to run again, not rightaway: the hell with it!

On the positive side, the reward money from the bank was sure helpful with projects like building the dam he needed on the tributary of the Spurlock River which snaked across his land. Not only could he now afford to buy all the materials needed, but he could hire labour to follow the rough plans he had drawn and start throwing up the log walls after the long, wearying days of excavations.

Yessir! That reward money had sure come in handy!

He was almost ready to concede that the publicity about his so-called heroism could be a mighty good thing after all, working positively for him, and it would have been if there hadn't been those years that he knew not everyone had forgotten, including some who would *never* want to forget.

Men from another time; remembering, vengeful....

The first sign he was right was a mysterious fire in his south-west pasture one balmy starry night, barely a week after the special edition of the *Gazette* had appeared. Flames roaring across the dark sky had not only destroyed the grassy pastures he had been nurturing for winter, but had burned much of the stacked building materials for his dam and the corrals he had planned. Even the shack containing his tools had been reduced to ashes, leaving a strong odour of coal oil behind.

He learned that reward money, no matter how welcome and useful, was no good for extinguishing fires, or stopping masked raiders from tearing down his fences and stampeding his herds straight for the big drop over the appropriately named Deadfall Cliffs.

Forty-three steers had died, or had had to be shot to put them out of the misery of horrific injuries. Hell! His herd only numbered about 120 head. A couple more raids like that and he would be out of business! But they had yet to find out just how stubborn he could be.

The Grantland sheriff, Casey McCall, was a tough, experienced lawman. He rode in while Buckley was still burning some of the carcasses scattered at the base of the cliffs. Pungent smoke swirled up and he sniffed exaggeratedly.

'Kinda reminiscent of roast beef, but I don't care for mine so well done,' he remarked, spitting.

Buckley wiped sweat and dirt from his brow, tugged down the neckerchief he had tied about his lower face and retorted, 'I'd like to cut you a steak, Casey, then slap you across the face with it!'

The sheriff, leaning forward slightly, hands folded over his saddlehorn, stiffened, then nodded solemnly.

'Yeah. Guess it wasn't all that funny. Sorry, Buck, but – seems you got some enemies.' He gestured to the mutilated steers, lifting his voice in a query.

'Looks that way.' No point in denying the obvious.

'Right after your picture appeared in the *Gazette*....' The lawman let the words hang.

Buckley looked at him bleakly. 'Never connected the two,' he said slowly. 'Dunno why anyone would.'

'Aw, was talkin' to Clip Harrow. You know, the cameraman? Yeah, 'course you do. He said he thought you was gonna slug him when he took your picture. I kinda had that same impression – that's why I had a word with him.'

Buckley kept silent, his face immobile.

McCall smiled thinly. 'I been totin' a badge for almost thirty years. You get to figure out a lot of things just by the way a man looks, or how he speaks under certain conditions, and I see you – close-up – when you first saw your picture takin' up most of the front page of the *Gazette*.

'Well, you managed to squeeze in, Case. That was your idea, wasn't it?'

The lawman's thin smile widened slightly. 'Another thing that makes me wonder, too, is how some folk try to change the subject, or at least divert it from the main topic, when they don't want to talk about somethin' that bothers 'em, or makes 'em uneasy.'

Buckley's eyes were wary now, but his jaw was set hard. 'That what you think I'm tryin' to do?'

McCall lifted a hand. 'Hold it. Whether you are or ain't tryin' to get me started on a discussion along them lines, I ain't interested. You know what I'm askin'; but I'll spell it out if you want: you did not want your picture spread all over that newspaper, did you? Oh, I seen it in your face. You afraid someone was gonna recognize you? Mebbe under some other name than Buck Buckley, which if you don't mind me sayin' so, is a pretty stupid name to choose if you don't want folk wonderin' about your real one. Got a kinda schoolboy touch to it, ain't it? Frivolous.'

Buckley's face was flushed now and his eyes were narrowed. A few muscles worked briefly along his jawline and then he sighed, and said, 'Had the same thought myself. But if anyone gets nosy, I'll just make a joke about it. Feeble, mebbe but....' He shrugged.

The sheriff stared silently for a short time, then nodded once. 'You know my next question.'

'I do?' Buckley's eyebrows arched.

'Don't get me mad, Buck! Or whatever your real name is!'

'Oh! That's what you're askin' me – my real name? Well, it's Adam Miles Buckley, but most of my life I've been called Buck....' His voice trailed off as he watched the anger build in the lawman.

'Don't get smart with me! I warned you!'

Buckley spread his hands. 'You asked me a question and I answered it.'

'Sure! With a mouthful of smart talk!'

Buckley sighed and shrugged. 'I can only tell you—'

'What you think I'll accept! Well, I'll tell you – what I want to hear is the truth! And, damnit, yeah, I'll even tell you why.'

Buckley could see the contained fury in the man, increased it by acting only mildly interested. 'I'm listenin', Sheriff. Not that I got any choice, huh?'

'How'd you like to listen through the bars of my cells?' gritted McCall.

'Don't entice me much, but I'd wonder what reason you'd use to lock me up. I mean—'

'I know what you mean, you sassy damn Reb!'

Buckley couldn't help but grin. 'Hell, Casey, you're reachin' back a long way if you figure that name'd get me riled!'

McCall stared, steam almost coming out of his ears and then his shoulders slumped and he grinned wryly.

'Yeah. I was kinda reachin', wasn't I? But, listen, I know Buckley ain't your real name. Yeah, yeah, how do I know, you're wonderin'? Just a hunch. That may not be good enough but it'll have to do for now. See, couldn't help wonder why a feller as popular as you suddenly got all stiff an' touchy about your picture in the paper when most folk would be happy to see themselves in that position.'

'I guess I'm just shy.'

McCall's weathered face hardened. 'You're just makin' this worse, you damn fool! Mebbe if I could match that picture to one on a Wanted dodger...?' He arched his eyebrows again and let the words hang.

'If you got the time to waste, lots of luck,' was all Buckley said, and there was absolutely no indication whether the man was simply dismissing the suggestion light-heartedly, or telling the lawman in a roundabout way to mind his own damn business.

McCall almost started to reach for his gun but changed his mind. 'I'll find out, Buck! You can bet on that.'

'Lemme know how you go,' Buckley said, as McCall stormed away, the big shoulders' stiffness reflecting his anger.

Then the sheriff stopped and whirled around. 'You know, I've had a few calls – oh, over a series of weeks, nothing pesky about 'em, they weren't complaints exactly – but they all said the same thing: there was a lot of shootin' comin' from your place – a few days apart, even a week, sometimes.'

Buckley kept his face blank, waiting.

'Yeah, well, I come out to check one time and I got me a pair of field-glasses, topped-out on that grassy hill.' He jerked his head in the general direction of the ranges. 'It was you doin' all the shootin' – practisin'. Just bustin' the hell outa targets like empty bottles, broken coffee mugs, all the way down to pebbles no bigger than pigeon's eggs. Just blastin' all hell outa 'em ... an' no misses that I saw.'

'Must've been one of my good days.'

The lawman snorted. 'One of your *very* good days, I'd say. Buck, you reminded me of a gunfighter keepin' in practice. That a fair enough description?'

'We-el, could be, I s'pose. 'Cept I'm no gunfighter.'

'I'm gonna reserve my opinion about that. Weren't no altar boy put down German Jack an' his men.'

'Mebbe a lotta luck helped.'

'Just possible, I guess. But—'

'You gonna stay for a cup of java, Casey? Or you ready to go?'

Their eyes met: not exactly with hostility, but in the sheriff's case, more like a wariness.

'Figure I better take the hint,' he said gruffly. ' So, I'll skip the coffee and get on my way.'

'Stop by anytime, Case, you know that.'

'Oh, I will. Have to wonder though: why didn't you report this to me?' He gestured to the bawling, mutilated and dead cattle.

Buckley didn't look fazed in any way. 'You're enough of a cattleman to see why cleanin'-up took priority, Case.'

McCall grunted and looked resigned.

'Got an answer for everything, ain't you?'

Buckley smiled faintly. 'Wish I did.'

Sheriff Casey McCall nodded curtly. 'Yeah. I'll check from time to time, just to see everythin's all right … suit you?'

'Make it so there's time for coffee, OK?'

Buckley watched impassively as the lawman rode

away.

'I know you'll be back, Casey,' he said quietly as he turned back to his unappetizing chore. 'Know damn well you will! You're like one of them terriers they train to catch rats. You just won't let go.'

CHAPTER 3

AVENGERS

The cattle raid and the fire were only the beginning.

Buckley had expected that, lost a good deal of sleep by camping out near the herds and, one night, on a ridge that overlooked the dam site.

He had made a slow ride around the area, checking it all out, a mite jumpy at sounds of night animals, actually shooting once when he saw – or thought he saw – a shadow just where he had heard a twig snap, or a sound very like it.

His bullet blew a squealing squirrel out of a tree as it clambered after some morsel. He kicked the poor torn little carcass under a bush and cursed himself for being so trigger-happy.

Get a hold of yourself, man! He gritted. Keep on like this and next thing you'll be barricading yourself in the ranch house, rigging coffee cans with stones in them on strings across doorways and windows....

'Well,' he said aloud, 'it's been a long time since that sort of thing was necessary and I don't want it to start again. No, sir!'

His apprehension was not without cause.

Back at the gory scene of the dead cattle, aiming to blow down a couple of sections of the Deadfalls to cover the bodies, someone took a shot at him.

He had just lit the short fuse on the dynamite charge he had planted under an overhang of rock and dirt when the bullet whacked into the bulge, bare inches from the sizzling dynamite fuse.

He was flat on his face in seconds, six-gun already in hand, hammer cocked under his thumb. Even as he scanned the trees on the top of the Deadfalls he figured whoever had fired at him could have been aiming at the drifting swirls of smoke from the sputtering fuse.... In which case the dynamite would have exploded and buried him under a couple of tons of rock and dirt ... a perfect cover-up in more ways than one.

So he rolled away quickly, dropped over a small ledge and thrust to his feet, running to a safe distance, and two more bullets followed him. One made him jerk his head it went so close to his ear, and the second tore a handful of bark from a tree he was making for at about head level.

Nice shooting, he thought tightly as he threw himself into cover and yet another bullet whined off the branch of a tree above him.

Then the dynamite blew with choking clouds of

dust and the rumble of disintegrating bulge.

He used the dust for cover to get to higher ground but still within the trees. He blotted sweat above his eyes with his shirt sleeve, wishing he had his rifle rather than just the six-gun, squinting as he searched the ridge where the shooter had been holed up; he could see the rising gunsmoke still hanging in the air up there. Even as he watched it began to drift off and he strained to see into the shadows beneath it.

There! Dulled sunlight penetrated the dust and trailing gunsmoke enough to flicker along the metal of a rifle barrel. He snapped a shot instantly, although it was a long range for a pistol. And he was a mite surprised to see a small, pale explosion of bark from a tree he had figured the bushwhacker would use as cover and likely a rest for his rifle.

Then there was a peculiar sound!

It came from where he had decided the shooter must be, but he didn't know what to make of the slightly high-pitched – what? A half-smothered, startled cry...?

Hell! He really didn't know what it was, some kind of animal maybe, but he triggered two more shots, saw leaves erupt, and twigs and bark fly.

There was identifiable sound this time, a sound someone would make crashing through the brush at the base of those trees.

The shooter making a run for it.

Had to be: no other explanation. He was already up and dropped down a few feet from the small rise where he was. One leg gave way briefly, throwing him off balance, and he dived for the ground, stretching out flat. But no more bullets came his way. The killer was too busy making his own escape.

Angry that he should have been bushwhacked on his own land, Buckley turned and ran for where he had left his horse, ground-hitched. He vaulted into the saddle, slapping the reins free, kicking his heels into the startled animal's flanks, wheeling sharply and jumping it off the ledge. The jar was considerable and he slid sideways as he hadn't yet settled firmly in the saddle, rammed his boots deeper and more securely into the stirrups and—

'*Too blasted late!*'

That summed it up: he could clearly hear the other mount gathering speed as the rider went up over the rise. He had several trees to negotiate before he came to the top, then had to ride around a thick patch of brush. He actually glimpsed the killer – no! Not really—

What he glimpsed was the killer's horse flashing between the bushes as he rode and weaved down into a draw Buckley hadn't known was there. About all he could tell was the killer forked a buckskin mount and was crouching low, wearing darkish clothes. No time to notice anything more.

'Must be at least two hundred damn' buckskins in this valley!' he told himself bitterly. Whoever it was, was going to get away with the attempt on his life. For now, maybe … just for now!

He reined down, patting his own mount's sweating neck.

Hit and run, the tactics of a coward, or someone who figured to try again…?

He half-smiled, already seeing Casey McCall's hard face staring at him in disbelief when he reported the attempt on his life.

Just for the hell of it!

'You take time to look for any tracks?' the sheriff asked curtly. 'Or you just run for cover?'

'I looked, Case. Nothing much to find. He knew the country, I guess. Made his run through a grove of trees where the leaves and twigs were inches deep. You could see where he'd ridden, but there were no clear hoofprints.'

McCall arched his heavy eyebrows and nodded thoughtfully. 'Well, now you know for sure you do have an enemy.' Then he added edgily, 'Even if you didn't before.'

'Well, I've dutifully reported it to the local representative of the law, now, haven't I? Make a note of that, too, will you, Case?'

McCall's look was not an amiable one. 'I will!'

Buckley spread his hands. 'Just doing like you asked, Case.'

'All right! You've done it. No need to wait.'

'Was gonna buy you lunch and a drink before I go back to work. Think I owe you one.'

'Some other time. Buck, no need for us to go

headbuttin' each other, but you *know* it was that picture in the Gazette that brought someone after you. Has to be.'

'It's ... possible.' Buckley didn't sound too sure.

'Which means someone recognized you from somewhere and seems to have a score to settle.'

'Could look at it that way,' he admitted slowly.

McCall's jaw hardened. 'Don't give an inch, do you! So I don't expect you'll tell me about any troubles you've brought with you to my bailiwick...? The ones your picture must've reminded someone of...?'

Buckley said nothing for a moment, then shrugged. 'Reckon you've got things mixed up, Case.'

'About what I expected you'd say. But lemme tell you this: if you've brought killer trouble into my territory I won't stand for it. I'll move you on so fast—'

Buckley started to turn away. 'Well, you do what you figure you have to, Casey. It don't mean I need to agree with you.'

'Hey! You come back here! Goddammit, Buck! I'm the Law here and what I say goes!'

Without turning, Buckley lifted a hand in acknowledgement and went out, leaving Casey McCall half-risen out of his chair but swearing only at the closed door.

He sat down with a thump and, still glaring at the office door, reached into the second drawer down in his battered desk and brought out a carefully folded copy of the *Gazette*.

He spread it out before him, then carefully folded it

so only the half-page picture of Buck Buckley showed.

'By God! I know I've seen you somewhere before. Or somethin' written about you with your picture starin' back at me.' He suddenly flicked the paper with the knuckles of his right hand and it tore right across Buckley's features. 'I'll remember. Sooner or later, I'll remember. Can't be too many men who could take on six bank robbers with just a Colt, and walk away without even a scratch! It'll come back to me and I ain't too sure I'm looking forward to that happening.'

It was after dark when Buck Buckley returned to his ranch house – dog-tired, yawning, every muscle aching.

He had been working this spread alone most of the time he had been here. He had hired local labour when he really needed it – and *needed* had to be stressed, because he was strapped for ready cash, or had been until the bank gave him that reward. He'd even taken part-time ranch work at round-up time to see him through.

Now that he had the reward money, things could get a lot easier. No more hard-scrabble deal running the spread alone, or trying to rake up the money necessary to pay for casual help, or pledge his time to some local rancher who had supplied some help, lending his own muscles for a day or two to work off the debt. Never the best arrangement!

But it was a good valley: folk here co-operated like that, one helping out the other when needed. He knew the folk hereabouts figured him just a mite strange because he didn't socialize as much as the others, but he didn't mind. He was quiet, taciturn, but painfully honest; paid his debts promptly, and that counted in Grantland County.

That was partly why there had been so much surprise when he had walked into that bank and shot down the robbers. No one had ever seen him use a six-gun in anger before, and those who had seen the brief, violent action in the bank were still talking about it in awed whispers.

'Never seen him draw or nothin'! The dang gun was just … there, blazing away in his hands and the robbers were fallin' on top of one another!'

Of course, there had been much talk afterwards when he hadn't wanted his picture taken but that crazy *Gazette* cameraman had got it anyway and printed it. There were some mighty wild theories about what made him so reticent but most were whispered if he was anywhere in sight.

'On the run from some crime …' was the favourite.

'Too damn honest for that!' was the popular counter.

'A woman's chasin' him – nothin' surer.'

'Ah, he's just one of them fellers don't talk much, sure not about hisself – but there could be a mean streak in there. Got that look about his mouth sometimes – an' his eyes! Way they pinched down when Luke Mayhew at the saloon told him he owed another dollar for his drinks – whew! I tell you, I was standing three men away and I got clear down to the end of the bar when he called Luke a lyin' thief.' The talker had shaken his head. 'Luke started to reach for his bung-starter, then stopped dead, with one hand under the counter when he looked up an' found Buck leanin' across, just starin' down at him, not sayin' a word. Needed to change his pants, I reckon! No, I ain't exaggeratin'! But I tell you, Luke knew he was close as dammit to findin' out how comfortable a coffin is.'

There was always such talk about taciturn men who went about their business in a quiet, easy manner, and didn't talk about themselves – or other folks' shortcomings either.

Buck was honest, as everyone knew, generous to the kids walking around the town with holes in their britches – seemed to get along right well with the town ladies, too, though no one had ever seen him going into any of their rooms. There was just that faint air of mystery, which, as it so often does, sparked all kinds of wild theories about his actions.

But he just kept on going about his ranching with some success, was still polite to the ladies and anyone he knew when he passed them in the street, and this made him more popular with the female population that the male.

The other thing that fazed the gossips and folk who were just genuinely curious about Buck Buckley, was that he didn't seem to care what they thought of him, one way or the other.

The news that someone had tried to shoot him, not long after burning his dam site and running his herd off a cliff, really got the theorists working over-time. But he still showed that overall indifference and no one could say he was any the less polite – nor more forthcoming. Just set about putting things to rights with a small crew he hired – two of the part-timers he occasionally used. They seemed happy enough to go on Buckley's payroll. Just the same, he was still the kind of mystery man who could spark a whole slew of wild theories.

And now it seemed that the *Gazette*'s front-page picture had stirred up something from his past that just might affect the whole blamed town. As the Doomsday gossips loved to speculate, he must have *something* in his past that could well bring avengers prowling the usually peaceful streets of Grantland.

No one wanted to see that.

So he had to get used to occasional hostile stares where none had been before and sometimes mothers quickly grabbing their children and crossing to the other side of the street.

Folk still liked him and even felt some sort of concern for his safety, but no one openly offered to help. It would have been refused, anyway, so he found himself pretty much a loner, amongst one-time friends who no longer crossed the street to exchange a few words … just gave a wave, and let it go at that.

And, of course, there the wild theories about just what his secret could be – on the run was top of the list, that went without saying, but from what gave much cause for speculation.

'Robbery's my guess – that'd explain how he was able to buy his spread in the first place.'

'Might've killed a man – or several – after we seen how he massacred German Jack and his crew. No one I know ever seen anyone use a Colt the way he did.'

'Yeah! Gunfighter for sure. Could have a whole slew of fellers after him.'

'Mebbe someone better ask the sheriff to tell him to kinda move on...?' was suggested.

'Yeah! Well away from here.'

A silence that dragged a couple of minutes. Then: 'They're pretty good friends, Casey McCall an' Buckley,' a townsman allowed mildly, and ...

That was where that particular discussion ended.

Buckley was just finishing shoeing his bay gelding when the lawman rode into his cluttered ranchyard.

'Wouldn't feel like fixin' a set of shoes for my old paint, I s'pose?' the sheriff asked, and automatically adjusted his gunbelt as soon as he dismounted.

Buckley straightened with a grunt, reaching around to briefly massage his lower back. 'Not today.'

McCall showed a half-smile as he let his sweating horse's reins trail.

Buckley gestured to the shaded water trough. 'When he's cooled down.... You been ridin' him hard for some reason?'

There was a hint of tension in Buckley's voice as he studied the lawman who thumbed back his hat and took out a somewhat crumpled pack of cheroots. He tossed one to the rancher, flipped one dexterously into his own mouth and walked forward, scraping a vesta across the left hip of his corduroy trousers.

With both smokes glowing, McCall looked into Buckley's face.

'Was two men in the saloon yesterday askin' after you.'

Buckley's face remained impassive as he drew on the cheroot. 'Say who they were?'

McCall shook his head briefly. 'They wore tied-down holsters, and the local drinkers made plenty of space for 'em at the bar without even havin' to be asked.'

Buckley nodded. 'Some fellers are like that; don't need to speak, you just know damn well to stear clear.'

'Seems to work that way. Didn't seem too pleased when that new barkeep said you weren't in town far as he knew. They'd be better off lookin' for you at your ranch.'

Buck took a long drag and spoke as he exhaled, the smoke dancing and breaking up with his words. 'I guess they wanted to know how to find my place.'

'They did. You – er – haven't seen 'em?'

'No one showed up looking for me.'

'Not quite what I asked....'

Their gazes met and Buckley suddenly clicked his fingers. 'Not unless – aw, wouldn't be, surely!'

The sheriff was tensed now. 'I ain't in any mood for games, Buck!'

The rancher lifted a hand, one finger extended.

'No games, Case. But Stew Downey's been bronc-bustin' for me, temporarily. You know Stew, don't you…?'

'Yeah! I damn well know him! The three of us've shared drinks often enough.'

Buck nodded calmly. 'Sure. Well, Stew thought he saw a couple of riders up on my north ridge, kinda keeping to the trees so they wouldn't be seen, and where I've got a few dozen head I'm fattening up for the market in Ringo Junction. A couple more weeks and I figure to get a mighty good price.'

'I'm happy for you!' gritted the sheriff impatiently. But let's get back to those two gunslingers who were lookin' for you.'

'I was getting' to them. Stew rode down to where I was planing a couple of planks for a new toolshed and told me he thought those riders might be scouting the herd.'

'Now I wonder how that idea jumped up and hit him in the face! Goddammit, Buck! You're gonna tell me you had a shoot-out with them fellers, ain't you.'

Buckley arched his eyebrows. 'Well you figured that out fast enough! What I was gonna say was, those damn rustlers just might've been the same ones who'd been looking for me.'

'And they found you – right?'

'Well, Stew was right, they were after my herd. When I yelled out, they started shootin' and we traded some lead, of course. I was coming in to tell you, Case, but my mount threw a shoe and I figured I might's well renew 'em all while I was about it.' He looked steadily at the tight-faced lawman.

'And...?'

The rancher shrugged. 'They're dead. Got their bodies all wrapped up nice and neat in some old canvas in yonder shed and—'

'All ready for burial! Or were you gonna drop 'em off the Deadfalls an' give the coyotes a feast!'

Somehow, Buckley managed to keep a reasonably innocent expression.

'Aw, now, Case! I was gonna bring 'em in to you.'

'Mebbe! Or mebbe not! After I'd told you that if you tangled with any more *hombres* comin' after you, I'd have to think about movin' you on!'

Buckley frowned. 'Did you say that, Case?' He shook his head slowly. 'Don't reckon I recall that part.'

'You know damn well I wouldn't have any choice! Even spelt it out that I wouldn't let our town be put in danger by anyone who'd seen that damn picture and realized it was one of someone on their kill-list! You ain't that good a friend I could let you endanger the whole blamed town.'

Buckley was nodding slowly now as he looked steadily at the sheriff. 'I sort of do recall somethin' like that, now you mention it, Case. Also, recollect I said I wouldn't run out and leave my spread. Taken me too damn long to get around to building it up – something I really wanted to do.'

For a moment, Casey McCall's grizzled face relaxed, just a fleeting reaction, but clearly evident. 'Yeah, I know … I figured you were tryin' hard to shake some-thin' from your past an' I was willin' to give you a break when I seen how hard you were workin' at doin' it. Till the *Gazette* spread you picture all over the County – I didn't count on that. It's already brought snakes outa the woodwork and I won't stand for that. I aim to keep this town safe and law-abidin', Buck … you know that.'

He paused, obviously waiting for Buckley to help him out but the rancher said nothing, kept his face as devoid of expression as he could.

The sheriff sighed. 'Looks like I was wrong. Oh, not about your past catching up with you so much, but – you gonna gimme trouble now I'm about to *officially* move you on?'

'I can't just up and quit my ranch! You know that!'

'I know damn well you ain't gonna quit, so I'll have to do what I said as a half-joke a little while back: if you stay, it'll be in one of my cells.'

As he said the last word, his six-gun came up, cocked, the barrel pointed at Buckley's chest. 'No way I could miss if I pulled the trigger, Buck.'

Buckley's eyes held steadily to McCall's face.

'But *would* you…?'

'You're damn close to findin' out.'

'Ah, well, in that case….'

Languidly, Buckley lifted both hands.

CHAPTER 4

SITTING DUCK

Buck couldn't really believe that McCall was going to lock him up, but that's exactly what the sober-faced sheriff did.

'Keep you off the streets and we mightn't have to worry about someone shootin' you from a rooftop or somewhere,' Casey told him, as he turned the key in the lock of the barred door. 'Scarin' folk – if nothin' else.'

'Your concern for my safety is mighty touching, Case,' Buckley said sourly. 'But if I just stay out on my spread and work it, you'd get the same result.'

'What? You figure anyone really wanted to nail you, they'd go out to your ranch where you've only got a small crew instead of here?' As Buckley nodded briefly, eyes steady on the lawman, McCall pursed his lips. 'Might, too, I guess. But it's still bringin' undesirables into my bailiwick and I don't aim for that to happen.'

He started to turn away and then swung back,

looking at Buckley through the bars.

'You must have a notion *why* someone would come after you?'

Buckley merely stared back.

'Look, I dunno what's in your past, not all of it, least-ways, and I sure as hell can't help you if you don't tell me!' He waited but Buckley just went and sat down on the edge of the narrow bunk against the wall beneath the barred window that allowed the street sounds to come in with slanting beam of afternoon sunlight.

'How about a lantern in here, Case? It'll be dark pretty soon.' He gestured to the cigarette he had just rolled, adding, 'An' I can save on matches.'

'When it's dark, is when you'll get a lantern!' the lawman said shortly and, as he turned away and strode down the short, stone-walled passage, added, 'Mebbe!'

'You're all heart, Casey,' Buckley called after him, then swung his legs up onto the bunk, punched the shapeless lump that would serve as a pillow and lay down, fingers locked behind his head as he smoked slowly.

That damn picture!

Even getting rid of all that itchy, annoying facial hair hadn't done the job he hoped it would. Too many sharp eyes had seen through it and recognized his hard-planed features once it had gone.

He had hoped by now, even if someone thought they recognized him, that they would decide: 'No! Couldn't be him – not after all this time.'

Still, he oughtn't to be too surprised: the kind of

folk who would recognize him were those with l-o-n-g memories – and empty pockets. Once again, he wished he had kicked that damned camera to pieces – and, yeah! – the operator, too. He glanced up and was surprised how dark it was already, a few moving lights or reflections showing through the high-barred window. Then suddenly, there was a different, deeper shadow, and a dull reflection, suddenly moving, something poking through the bars, searching....

He threw himself off the bunk as the first two shots crashed and filled the cell with sound, the ricocheting bullets making him scrabble desperately to get under the bunk for protection.

The shooter emptied the six-gun in a ragged volley, bullets ripping through the worn blankets, splintering the bunk's low sides, a sliver of wood stinging Buckley's neck.

There was a pause as the booming echoes filled his head and he knew the shooter was hurriedly reloading. He lunged across the space between the bunk and the slab of wall directly beneath the barred window, huddling close.

Sure enough! The gun appeared again at the bars, seeking him, angling down when the killer realized he must be crouching directly below the window. He jumped aside as it fired, felt the heat of the powder-flash, heard the lead punch into a bunk leg.

Damned determined, this son of a bitch!

Suddenly, he jumped up and slapped at the smoking Colt. It tore loose surprisingly easily from the killer's hand, startling him. Then—

A stifled cry froze him briefly as he scooped the weapon up from the floor just as McCall's voice cracked at the big cell door. 'Drop it, Buck!'

With the sheriff's Colt menacing him, Buckley tossed the gun on the bunk, started to lift his hands, head cocked for sounds of the killer's getaway.

'Not goin' after him?' he asked tightly.

'He'd be home havin' supper by the time I got outa the cell block and around the side.' Then Buckley stood up straight, and McCall snapped, 'The hell're you doin'? I told you to leave that gun alone!'

Buckley straightened from the bunk, one hand stretched out towards the killer's six-gun. 'I need to pick it up, Case—'

'The hell you do!' McCall's gun hammer clicked to full cock.

'I ain't gonna try anything. It's just that – well, that gun smells.'

The lawman blinked, and then his jaw hardened. 'A gun that don't smell'd surprise me more.'

'Don't mean it smells of gun oil!' Buckley growled. 'Nor gun powder! It – it smells like a woman.'

'What in the hell's wrong with you! "Smells like a woman!" A six-gun that's just fired all its shots smells like—'

'Like a woman's purse!' Buckley cut in. 'Where they keep their face powder or mebbe a small bottle of perfume. And when they open it, you get this – lady smell.'

McCall started to snap a reply, but swallowed it and frowned. 'You sayin' some woman toted a couple of pounds of iron around in her handbag! Then gave it some Johnny to shoot at you through the bars?'

'I'm sayin' that I grabbed that gun from the killer's hand and it came away like I was takin' it from a kid – hardly any resistance. And now there's a smell of face-powder or somethin' like it, right here in the damn cell! Sniff! Unless you're wearin' somethin' sweet?'

'All right, all right! I can smell it, and it's just like you said: smells like a woman's handbag. But—'

'Told you there was almost no resistance when I grabbed it. You'd think a man would be hanging on tight, ready to shoot whenever I tried to move.'

The lawman remained silent for a short time.

'You figure it was a woman tryin' to shoot you, that what this is all about?'

'I'm saying that it points that way. Matter of fact, I think she might've tried once before. I tangled with someone on my land, and my shot went close. There was a kinda yelp, but I didn't recognize it as a woman's cry at the time. But now, with this, yeah! I reckon she's tried earlier.'

'You upset any ladies lately?'

'Not that I know of – they all kissed me goodbye when it came time for me to go.'

The sheriff stood there, frowning. 'Well, standin' here jawin' about it has given her – or him – or whoever – plenty of time to get away, and I've still got the problem of what I'm goin' to do with you. I thought puttin' you in here would be a good idea, but – well, now I ain't so sure.'

'All it did was make me a sittin' duck.'

The sheriff nodded slowly. 'Yeah, I guess I—'

'You made a mistake, Case! No guessin' needed. You figured that locking me up here would make anyone who had a mind to put a bullet in me stay away, keep your lousy town fee of "undesirables"! Instead, like I said, I'm a sittin' duck. Goddammit, Case, you could've got me killed!'

McCall looked at him impassively.

'Don't see no blood spurtin', but we'll move you, I reckon. Got an old storeroom underneath this buildin', be a bit smelly—'

'Sounds like I'll have all the comforts of home!'

'You'll have a blanket – *and* a lantern. Recall you asked for one?'

'I've got a suggestion what you can do with the lantern! But, listen, Case, if you'll let me go back to my spread, there'll be no problem. I've got a couple ranch hands now, you know, able to put 'em on permanent with the reward money for stopping the bank robbery. It's a good ways from your precious town and I can protect myself better there.'

'Too far away,' the lawman growled. 'Come on. The storeroom it is – for the night, anyway. We'll figure somethin' better in the mornin'.'

Buckley spread his hands in an 'I give up!' gesture as the sheriff unlocked the main door and stood to one side holding it, indicating with a jerk of his head for Buckley to come out.

Buck made a brief sucking sound through his teeth and slowly shook his head as he started past McCall – noting now that the sheriff was holding the door open with the edge almost touching his now holstered gun … making it mighty hard to draw the weapon! The sheriff had relaxed considerably, confident that Buckley would co-operate, but maybe he was just a mite too confident.

Casey McCall gave a sudden yell as Buckley slammed his shoulder into the edge of the door and jerked it hard. The lawman staggered but reacted much more quickly that Buckley expected. His right arm must have been throbbing from the iron edge of the cell door but his hand closed around the butt of his Colt and began to lift the weapon even as Buckley swung the door again on its well-oiled hinges.

The heavy iron edge caught McCall in the chest – and across the side of the head. He staggered back about three feet, started to go down fast. Buckley kicked at his legs to hurry the process and put the startled man on his back. He planted his boot in the middle of the sheriff's chest, pinning him, then stooped and picked up the Colt. As the dazed but recovering McCall tried to sit up, Buckley said, 'Sorry, Case. Folk always say you're hard-headed – I hope they're right!'

And he slammed the gun barrel against the lawman's head. As the dazed man collapsed, hat spilling off, Buckley grabbed him under the arms and heaved him through the door of the cluttered storeroom. He took the man's gun and cartridge belt – and the cell keys – and had the door locked in seconds. He started along the shadowed hallway to the office, tossing the keys onto McCall's cluttered desk.

Less than five minutes later, he was riding his own bay gelding out of town.

'Now he's really done it!' McCall muttered, and irritably pushed the doctor's hand away from the split in his scalp just in front of his left ear. 'Bustin' outa jail! Assaultin' a law officer – me!'

'Will you sit still!' snapped the exasperated medico, as he snipped off the third and final suture in the small gash. He held a wad of iodine-soaked cotton against it and McCall sucked in air sharply between his big teeth.

'It's superficial. The sutures are to stop any more bleeding, which might well add to your comfort, Sheriff.'

McCall grunted, touched the wound lightly and had his hand slapped away. 'Don't! You'll introduce dirt and—'

'All right, all right! Thanks, Doc. Can you gimme somethin' for this headache?'

'Certainly.' The greybeard medico took a folded paper from his bag and handed it to the lawman. 'Wash this powder down with half a glass of water – but don't try the same thing with this.'

'This' was another, slightly larger square of folded

paper and McCall looked at him puzzledly.

'Your bill, Casey! You are not exempt from paying for my services, you know.'

The lawman growled and stood up, swaying slightly. The doctor steadied him. 'Try to get a good night's sleep.'

'Sleep! You loco? I'm goin' after Buckley! He ain't gonna get away with ... this....' He staggered and was steadied once more by Dr Howard Gordon.

'Sit down! And you take my advice: get – some – sleep! You'll feel more like riding in the morning. Surely there's no rush? You know Buckley will go back to his ranch.'

McCall muttered a curse. 'Sure I do! But you ever been out there, Doc?' The sawbones frowned and shook his head briefly. 'Hell, he's got himself a big spread, you know. Not usin' all his land right now: some back up into them Breakback Ridges – and you know what they're like.'

'I – er – know their reputation for being rather formidable to penetrate.'

'One way of puttin' it. The land came as a package and them Breakbacks were part of it. He figures sometime to make use of them. Gonna experiment with cattle the Mexes breed to run in the Sierras. But, hell with that! What I'm sayin' is, there's a hundred places he can hide in there and no one – *no one* – will find him, and I include anyone who might be after his hide.'

'Like this – er – mystery assassin who tried to shoot him in his cell?'

'Yeah!' Casey McCall paused and looked squarely at the doctor who was still fussing with his bag and its contents. 'He thinks it could be a woman.'

The doctor swung around quickly, staring. 'A woman...?'

'Yeah. Thinks she already made a try out on his spread but run off when the goin' got tough.' McCall told how Buck thought it could have been a woman who made a half-strangled cry, but at the time couldn't be sure what the sound was.

Doctor Gordon looked thoughtful.

'You know, you told me about the gun smelling of perfume or face powder and how effortless Buckley thought it was to grab it through the bars – a weapon like that could easily put a strain on a woman's delicate wrist. She had already fired it several times, so her grip might've been weakened. Yes, yes! A woman could very well fit the bill!'

McCall muttered a half-smothered curse. 'I ain't never tangled with no woman.' Then he added hurriedly, 'Er, who was tryin' to kill someone, you unnerstand, Doc? I mean—'

The medic smiled and nodded. 'Be a new experience for you, then, Sheriff.'

'But it won't stop her from goin' down there to hunt him, if she's a mind, which is why I wanted him locked up safe, right here in my jail. Figured I could control things better from here, but with him livin' out there, him and them rough ranch hands he's hired, he could start a damn war if he wanted to.' He shook his head, plainly worried. '*And* he knows that country inside and out … better'n me.'

The doctor studied McCall's face and smiled slowly. 'You really do think of him more as a friend than an enemy, don't you, Casey? Oh, don't start blustering! You're a lot softer than you make out and I admire you for that.' He suddenly took the account paper from the sheriff's fingers and tore it up. 'You are a good lawman, Casey, but don't be too tough on Buckley. Let him see you do have his interests at heart. I believe he's a man who could use a really good friend right now. He already seems to have more enemies than he needs.'

The lawman was silent for a few heartbeats, then said, 'He saved my life once, so I guess I owe him somethin'.'

'Let him know it then,' the doctor said quietly. 'It's only fair, Casey. I've always believed you're a fair man – hard, when you need to be, but fair. There aren't many men you can say that about, not in this town, anyway. Now! Get – some – sleep! Please!'

McCall blinked and stared after the sawbones as he took his leave. Then he looked down at the torn pieces of the bill scattered around his boots.

'Guess that's one I owe you, Buck!'

CHAPTER 5

BUSHWHACK

Next morning, Doc Gordon, when he answered the door, was surprised to find the sheriff standing on his doorstep.

The lawman was holding a blood-spotted handker-chief to one side of his face, just above the left eye.

'What the devil have you done now?'

'Aw, I kinda sleep best on the left side, Doc. Musta rubbed it a mite too hard against my pillow, and felt this damn prick and next thing that gash you stitched up was bleedin' all over my bed.'

Gordon had ushered him into his office while he was talking, motioned him to a chair and, when the sheriff sat down, he moistened a clean rag in a bowl of antiseptic-smelling water, pushed the lawman's big, clumsy fingers aside and examined the wound.

'Yes, you've burst a stitch and torn the flesh a little more. I'll wash it with antiseptic and put a couple more sutures in – no great harm done.' He paused. 'I take it by your clothes and the glimpse I had of your horse outside your office that you are going – shall we say – a'hunting?'

'Sort of. I want to make sure Buck's gonna stay outa town. Can you kinda hurry it up, Doc? The stage is due in twenty minutes and I aim to check it out before I go.'

The medic paused, with his needle and gut an inch or so from the wound which was still seeping a little blood. The sheriff kept talking.

'It's the Saturday run comin' up from Rapid City. Always check it. Marshal down there has a habit of kickin' his drunks and troublemakers out and sendin' 'em up here to spend Saturdays.' He paused and gave a crooked smile. 'He don't much like me – not after I sent him a wild bunch of brawlin' saloon gals and one turned out to be his ex-wife who'd been lookin' for him to pay her money he owed.'

Gordon smiled. 'You do lead an interesting life, Casey. There, I've covered the wound with a strip of plaster. Should've done it in the first place … no charge.'

'You're a man to ride the river with, Doc,' McCall said on his way out, arranging his hat carefully so the band didn't touch the wound.

But he pressed it a little too hard and swore all the way to the depot, seeing by the settling dust cloud that the stage from Rapid City had just pulled in. He found his usual place in the doorway of the feed store opposite and carefully rolled a cigarette as he ran his eyes over the passengers now gathering around the stagecoach's boot where the sweating driver and his sidekick were unloading the luggage.

There was a mild fuss when someone was given the wrong bag and while it was being noisily sorted out, McCall finished his smoke, hitched his gunbelt, and strolled closer.

Settling his shoulders against the depot wall, he was just relaxing when he stiffened as he saw two of the passengers roughly jostling the others aside, ignoring complaints as they pushed past the protesting driver ill-manneredly, and grabbed two of the bedrolls.

'I'd've handed 'em to you in a couple of minutes, anyway, if you'd been patient!' the driver said grouchily.

The men ignored him and bulled a way through the small crowd – coming face to face with Casey McCall.

'Just take it easy, gents,' he said softly. 'We run a nice, orderly town here.'

The men looked at him, both unsmiling, both unshaven and hard-eyed, one with a full moustache. The other thinner man spat into the dust, close enough to McCall's boot to make him step back quickly. The movement swung his vest open and revealed his sheriff's star pinned to his shirt pocket.

'Oh-oh, Mike! We got us a lawman to welcome us.'

It was the one with the moustache who had spoken. Now the second man, face like an axeblade, and just about as friendly, prepared to spit again.

'Swallow that, mister, or you'll be swallowing lead!' McCall's hand dropped to his gun butt and the man glared back, then swallowed audibly, his prominent Adam's apple bobbing in his throat.

'Well, smoke me!' said his companion, moustache bristling briefly. 'Look who we got here! If it ain't good ol' Deputy McCall himself, all the way from Rapid City.'

'Looks like he's been promoted, Kel. An' see the polish on that brass star! Mighty proud of it, eh, Sheriff?'

'Just remember what it stands for. You two got business here? Murphy and Rainey, if I recollect?'

'Hell, he's got us dead to rights, Mike! Nice to see you again, McCall.'

'Don't bet on it. You got business in town, get done: but it better not be any of your bounty-huntin', savvy? The stage leaves at sundown.'

'Aw, don't care much for night travel – you, Kel?'

'Never have. Sheriff, we just want a good night's sleep – not right away, mind! – and we'll catch your noon stage out tomorrow. That suit you?' It sounded reasonable.

McCall took his time answering, but there was really only one thing to say without sounding like he was rawhiding these two: he saw some of the townsfolk watching, wondering just how tough he was going to be with the men. 'Make it an early night.'

Then he swung away and Mike Murphy looked at Kel Rainey and pursed his lips.

'S'pose we could, if we can find us a couple of accommodatin' ladies to keep us company...?'

'Aw, hell, why not? This ain't much of a town anyway. Be a pleasure to get on that noon stage, I reckon.'

McCall frowned as they shouldered their warbags and moved away across the street. They'd sounded accommodating, but McCall had already formed his own opinion.

Troublemakers – from way back.

And he knew damn well whose lap the trouble was going to land in now they were sticking around a spell.

But they behaved themselves – or, seemed to. Had a meal in the back room of the saloon, spent a little time with a couple of good-time gals, and then played a few hands of poker – Murphy winning some money, but Rainey coming away with a long face, starting to look mean as they headed for the bar.

But they did make an early night of it.

When McCall checked next morning he was told the pair had quit town before sun-up.

'Before! Say where they were going?'

'Not 'xactly, but the one with the moustache asked the way to Gauntlet Valley. Offered to pay ten bucks to anyone who'd show 'em the way. Then they asked about—'

McCall felt his belly muscles tense. 'Any takers?'

'I'm tryin' to tell you! Cleve O'Day said he'd do it. He's that drifter, works when he feels like it. Just finished a coupla days here and—'

'I know Cleve. Does a little carpentry, don't he?'

The saloon man smiled crookedly. 'Yeah, but he's gotta be really strapped before he'll take that on.'

'Did some work in that line for Buck Buckley, so he'd know the way out there. The saloon man may have noticed a tense sound in the sheriff's voice. 'Seem to recall Buck kicked his tail offa his place, last time. Caught him with a runnin'-iron. Yeah, he'd know the way there, all right, but he don't have any love for Buck.'

'Well, them strangers asked for him by name.'

The lawman was turning away as the saloon man spoke, and paused, swinging back quickly. 'Asked for Cleve?'

'Yeah. I started to tell you, but you jumped in too quick. Seemed like someone'd told 'em he'd be a good man to show 'em— Aw! You're welcome, Sheriff, any time!'

The saloon man said this last bitterly as the lawman hurried from the dim bar room without another word.

The sheriff had a lot of miles to make up.

Quitting town before daylight, and with a man like Cleve O'Day showing them the way, Murphy and Rainey would be on Buckley's land by – hell! Within the next hour, maybe less!

From what he knew about Cleve, the man would do just about anything to avoid having to actually work for his money. He had been around the area for a couple of years now, not in any real trouble, but just a little here and there – mostly brawls (usually over a woman), but he did shoot a man one time over a hand of poker he figured he'd been cheated out of – and he was right, as it turned out.

But McCall's general opinion of Cleve O'Day was that the man would bend the rules any way it suited him just to put a few easy bucks in his pocket. So, with a couple of hardcases like Rainey and Murphy more than likely offering good money for being shown a place where they could ambush Buckley, well, that kind of job would suit a man like Cleve O'Day.

Now all Sheriff Casey McCall had to do was find out where O'Day had taken Murphy and Rainey – *and do it before they bushwhacked Buckley.*

He rode hard, chancing a couple of short cuts that he wasn't too sure of and – to his surprise – found that they led him straight to Buckley's place.

He didn't see O'Day or any sign of Murphy and Rainey – obviously they had taken another way – but he figured the quicker he reached Buckley's place – by *any* way – the better.

He had to give his horse a blow and it gave him trouble, wanting to get at the creek it could hear trickling beyond the line of timber where he'd stopped. It was just as he lit a cigarette that he heard gunfire and he quickly trod it into the ground.

'Goddammit!' he breathed. 'Sounds like I'm too late!'

*

Buck Buckley swore when Jim Shorten, a replacement for one of injured top hands, came into the range camp leading his horse. It was limping, snorting and tossing its head.

'Hell! Don't tell me he's thrown a shoe!'

'That's what he's done, boss, I was—'

'I just did a heap of shoeing yesterday and if you'd come in when you were s'posed to, I'd've had a new set on your bronc by now!'

Shorten, a lanky man who did not live up to his name, flushed and moved uneasily. 'Well, I thought I seen that wild stallion with the crooked eye that's been stirrin' up the remuda, boss, an' – an' I went after him.'

'Find him?' Buckley asked tightly, and when Shorten shook his head, unable to meet his eye, said, 'That'd be up near the Reservation?' Shorten grimaced as he nodded. 'Uh-huh. Happen to see that l'il half-breed gal works in the office while you were ridin' that way?'

'Aw, I'm sorry, Buck. It – it weren't planned. Just thought I'd like to catch a glimpse of her. I did see her and—'

Buckley shook his head. 'Told you, you'll lose your scalp. Red Cloud's got her top of his list for his next wife. But I got no time to kick your stupid butt now. Here, take my hoss and get down to Shiloh's camp and bring back two cans of coal oil. I want a firebreak made before we call it quits for the day. Someone's gonna have to stay overnight and make sure the fire don't start up again and get outa hand, too – I ain't quite decided who yet, but—'

'I-I'll do it, Buck, but it's getting' kinda cold these nights and I ain't even got a jacket with me.'

Buckley merely slid a folded grey jacket from behind his saddle, held the reins of his bay gelding and pointed with the other hand towards the distant smoke that marked Shiloh's camp at the far end of the pasture.

'This'll fit. Thanks for volunteerin', Jim.'

'Er, is that what I done?'

'Sure did. You OK with that?' As if Shorten could do anything else but nod....

Buck half smiled as the chastened rider took the reins and handed over those of his own horse, a hard-worked sorrel.

A little later that day, when Cleve O'Day led Murphy and Rainey over the ridge, they stopped abruptly.

'Told you I smelled smoke down the trail apiece!' Rainey said, hauling his mount back just below the ridge top so he wouldn't be skylined.

There was a fire burning below, obviously lit deliberately, and with three riders keeping it confined to the limits they wanted. They were indistinct because of the drifting smoke, though one man seemed to be afoot, holding the head of his mount. They couldn't make out who through the swirling smoke.

'Hell! Can you see Buckley?' snapped Murphy, squinting.

O'Day said, 'Not close enough to be sure, but he forks a bay geldin' an'—There! To the left. Where that

rider in the grey jacket's leanin' down and draggin'
that bush away from—'

'I see the sonuver!' cut in Murphy tautly, unsheath-
ing his rifle. 'Kel, move a few yards round to your right
and we can get him in a crossfire.'

'Right!' Rainey hauled his mount around where
indicated, called in a low voice, but unable to disguise
the excitement he was feeling. 'I see him now! Smoke's
thinner here. I've got him, Mike! I – can – nail him!'

'Christ! Make sure!'

'I'm sure.'

'That's him, all right,' O'Day said, pointing.
'Crouchin' low over that bay. Best if you get him before
he reaches them trees.'

But Rainey was already dismounted, down on one
knee, rifle to his shoulder. Murphy was still in the
saddle, standing in the stirrups of his well-trained
mount, his own rifle rising to the ready position.

The guns fired a split second apart and the rider on
the bay gelding jerked and twisted as he was blown out
of the saddle, skidding and rolling wildly in the dust.

'Paid in full! You son of a bitch!' shouted Rainey
jubilantly.

'Er, not – not quite, gents....'

Murphy and Rainey turned quickly towards Cleve
O'Day who noticeably cringed as he stammered, 'Look
th-there!' He pointed with a shaky finger at the man
just straightening from checking for any obvious loose
horseshoes on a big stallion behind the bay, startled by
the gunshots.

'Th-that's Buckley!' gulped Cleve nervously. 'Couldn't see that other feller clearly. Think it was Jim Shorten. He musta borrowed Buckley's hoss and—'

By now Buckley, glancing grimly at the bush-whacked Shorten, quickly slid his rifle from the saddle scabbard and dropped flat beside the horse he's been checking. He rolled under a bush, squirmed around as lead peppered the foliage above him. He glanced again at the sprawled, unmoving cowhand, then brought the rifle up, levering and firing with eye-blurring speed.

Cleve O'Day, standing, pointing, went crashing backward, pumping legs unable to hold him as the bullet knocked him off balance. As he crashed to the ground, Buckley triggered two more fast shots and Rainey and Murphy dived for cover.

They were quick to return his fire but then ducked again, sprawling, as he raked their shelter, using every shot in his rifle's magazine. With the gunsmoke shrouding him and curling out of the muzzle, he ran for his mount.

'Judas Priest! He's fast!' allowed Murphy.

'I'll say!' panted Rainey, as Buckley threw himself at the saddle and, draped across it, yelled and ran the mount for a thin line of trees and beyond, into a wall of heavy brush.

He was so quick that he was well under cover before bullets rattled through the thin branches, seeking him.

And then he was gone....

'Well,' said Rainey, as grim-faced and tight-lipped, he looked at Cleve O'Day who was holding a blood-soaked kerchief against his left ribs. 'That was some successful ambush!'

'I-I never knew he was that quick!' Cleve gasped, blood dripping between his fingers. 'I-I think I've got a busted rib....'

'Lucky it ain't a busted head! You took our money!'

'Aw, now, wait up! I said I'd lead you to Buckley and I did! The-the shootin's up to you.'

'He's right, Kel,' said Murphy. 'Shootin's up to us.'

Then he swung his rifle towards Cleve whose eyes almost popped out of his head as he jumped back in sudden panic. 'No, listen, I can—'

The rifle whiplashed twice and Cleve O'Day was slammed over backwards, slid a little way down the short slope, rolled onto his face and was still.

Rainey looked uncertainly at Murphy who shrugged.

'That damn Buckley! Talk about a dead shot!'

He looked down at the sprawled O'Day and shook his head slowly, then lifted his hard gaze to Rainey. 'A *very* good shot – our friend Buckley, eh?' He winked and Rainey smiled slowly.

'Oh, yeah! Mighty dangerous character, all right. He don't hesitate to shoot to kill!'

Murphy nodded solemnly. 'McCall ain't gonna like this though. An' he don't like us, neither.'

'Figure he'll come down on us?'

'And hard, if he lives up to his rep.'

Rainey frowned, glancing at O'Day's body. Then he swung up his rifle and fired three fast shots into the dead man, the body jerking with each hit.

'You gone plumb loco?' shouted Murphy. 'Christ! McCall finds all them bullets in him an'—!'

'Yeah, that Buckley! Din' know when to stop. Like he wanted to blow poor old Cleve clear off the planet.'

'Aw, I see-ee,' Murphy said slowly. 'Buckley, huh?'

'Hell, yeah! He went loco soon as he seen Cleve'd led us to him, emptied what was left in his magazine and blew Old Cleve all over the countryside. I mean, hell! We din't come lookin' for no shoot-out, did we? Dunno about you, but it's sure shook me up.'

He was staring hard into Rainey's face and watched the slow, understanding smile being to spread across those axeblade features.

'Someone's gonna get his ass kicked!'

'Well an' truly, but it ain't gonna be us.'

CHAPTER 6

TOO MANY BULLETS

Sheriff Casey McCall saw the two riders below where he sat his mount on the ridge.

He recognized them easily enough, but wondered who was the dead man Murphy was leading on a horse he didn't recall seeing before. The man had to be dead: he could see the blood-soaked, bullet-torn jacket from here. The corpse was hatless and the way that lank, almost colourless hair dangled, the lawman figured it just had to be Cleve O'Day. No one else he knew had hair like that – untidy, unkempt, like short lengths of pale rope unraveling.

'It sure as hell ain't Buck,' McCall murmured aloud with a trace of relief. He took one more look around to make sure Buckley wasn't anywhere around but – no sign of him.

The shooting he had heard had come from a long way back, possibly even beyond that other ridge.

Anyway, he'd better get the straight of what he was seeing now, so he drew his Colt and triggered a single shot that had the riders below hauling quickly on their reins, looking up sharply to where he sat – openly now – on the ridge.

'Wait right there!' he bellowed, as he urged his horse down the slope.

Murphy and Rainey waited uneasily, but when he rode up, they greeted him affably enough, trying to seem at ease.

'Ah, Sheriff!' said Murphy. 'Bit of luck. You'll save us a ride all the way into town.' He gestured casually to the dead man draped over the horse Rainey was leading. 'Present for you – courtesy of your friend Buckley.'

Rainey hauled the third horse around so the lawman could get a better look at its burden.

McCall set his bleak gaze on their faces, moving it from one side to the other, his own face grim. 'Yeah. Figured it was Cleve by the hair. You say Buck Buckley killed him?'

'*Killed* him!' Rainey almost spat. 'Jesus, McCall, *look* at him! Buckley butchered him. Like shot him to pieces, at least five or six bullets, I reckon.'

Murphy nodded emphatically. 'Yeah! Blew old Cleve all to hell an' gone.'

McCall was frowning deeply now. 'You're tellin' me Buck Buckley tore up O'Day like this? Sure don't sound like him. He's a one shot man – a dead shot!'

They didn't like being under that cold, accusing scrutiny, but both men nodded.

'Yeah, he's a good shot all right,' Rainey admitted. 'Nailed Cleve with his first bullet then opened up before Cleve even hit the ground. Pumped another four or five into him … Geez! I tell you, it shook me!'

'Me too,' cut in Murphy. 'I mean, anyone could see Cleve was already dead and fallin'….'

'Yeah,' agreed Rainey, grimacing. 'But I guess someone who can shoot down half-a-dozen men in a few seconds….' He paused, shrugged, 'Well, killin'd come easy to someone like that, I reckon.'

'Still ain't like Buck, but I take your point.' McCall paused long enough to see the relief on their faces. Then, still sounding casual, added, 'Tell you what, you gents mosey on into town with Cleve anyway. Take him to Doc Gordon and tell him I want an official death certificate – a *detailed* one – statin' exact cause of death.'

Murphy snorted. 'A blind man can see *how* he died, for Chris' sake!'

'Do – what – I – told – you,' Sheriff McCall said flatly, each word a hammer-blow. 'I'll be in town shortly and we can go into it some more.'

'Well, hell, I don't see what we have to go into!' growled Rainey but, catching the look on the lawman's face, added hurriedly, 'But if that's what you want, Case….'

'It is. Now get a move on.'

'Jesus, what's the hurry?' Murphy began then nodded quickly. 'Yeah, yeah, on our way, Case, on our way!'

As they started off, Rainey called over his shoulder, 'Doubt you'll find Buckley still hangin' around.'

'Let me worry about that. Now *move*! And you be waitin' in my office when I get back.'

'Thought you wanted us outa town—' Rainey started, then, when McCall's right hand lightly caressed his gun butt, added quickly, 'Halfway there already, Case!'

'Judas, McCall!' said Murphy. 'We ain't done nothin' wrong! We're tryin' to help you, an' you're ridin' us.'

'You wanna help? Then – do – like – I – say!'

That tone and the lawman's hand now curled around the gun butt got them moving.

He let them go several hundred yards, then, with a wry grin, started after them.

Rainey glanced around, stiffened in the saddle, must have said something to Murphy who also wrenched around, jaw dropping as he watched the lawman riding along casually, not closing the distance: but there was no doubt he was following them.

Never hurt to make a couple of hardcases like Rainey and Murphy feel a mite uneasy, the sheriff told himself.

The fact was, he had known Buckley a long time, but had never seen or heard of him shooting a man more than once, which was usually enough, Buck being such a good marksman. Just ask anyone who had seen what he did to German Jack and his bank robbers. Six shots – six seconds – six dead men. A bullet apiece. Seemed to Casey McCall that there were far too many bullets in Cleve O'Day. Far too many.

*

He didn't close the gap, let the two men and their burden ride at about the same distance all the way and grow more and more edgy as the slow miles passed.

Rainey even rode back once and called from the bottom of a rise, 'Somethin' else you want, Casey?'

'Nope. Just decided to come on in. Keep goin'. You can have the doc workin' on Cleve before I get there.'

Rainey gave him a sort of smile – more of a grimace – then nodded and spurred his mount across to where Murphy waited. The seemed to have a few words, then turned and continued on their way, hurrying now, no longer looking back.

McCall took time to pack a pipe and smoke it by a shaded bend of the small stream the locals called Piss Creek, because, in truth, it was little more than a trickle.

When he eventually reached town, he went to the general store, bought some tobacco, a fresh pack of cheroots for when he was too busy to stop and roll a smoke, and some coffee beans which he would grind later.

He was a mite surprised when he finally rode into his street – a short, dead end – and saw Doc Gordon waiting on his landing, looking a little anxious – 'anxious' for the medic, anyway.

'Case,' Gordon greeted him quietly.

'Howdy, Doc,' the lawman said, swinging down stiffly from the saddle. 'Them two idiots leave you locked out?'

'No, no. I've examined O'Day's corpse. Wanted a

word with you.'

'Too many bullets?' the lawman asked, opening his door and gesturing for the medic to enter.

'Well, there were certainly more than was needed to kill him, but the odd thing is that four – maybe five – of those wounds have hardly bled at all. In fact, I'd say any blood they showed, just oozed out.'

'Not quite with you, Doc.'

'The other wounds, the two that actually killed him – well, they bled plenty, as you'd expect. Are you with me yet?'

McCall frowned for a moment or two, then looked up sharply. 'You're sayin' the ones that *didn't* show signs of a lot of bleedin' were—?' The medic said nothing, just looked hard until McCall nodded – just once. 'Shot into him *after* he was already dead. That it?'

'Yes. Probably just a short time later, but long enough for Cleve's blood pressure to completely fail. Nothing left then to move any blood through his veins.'

McCall's grim face hardened even more as he dropped a hand to his gun butt and jerked his head towards his inner door.

'Rainey and Murphy still in there?'

'I wouldn't swear to it, Casey. I told them they ought to wait to see you, but they sensed there was something wrong.'

McCall was already moving, shouldering open the office door, seeing immediately the narrow rear door swinging open on its hinges.

He swore softly, hurrying back past Doc Gordon.

'You might've tried to stop 'em, Doc!'

'Would you care to help me do an appendectomy on Chet Levine, Sheriff? I'm on my way there now.'

McCall stopped dead, frowning. 'The hell you talkin' about? You know I couldn't do – ah! Yea, OK. I get it, Doc. Chet Levine's your kinda job....' His voice trailed off and he looked sheepish. 'And Rainey and Murphy are my kind. Thanks anyway for pickin' up on them extra bullets.'

'I think Rainey knew what I was getting at about the lack of bleeding. Maybe Murphy did too.'

'They'd know, all right! Murderin' bastards! Be lucky if I catch up with 'em this side of the big range now.'

McCall was already on his way out the rear door as he flung the words over his shoulder, hurrying towards the small stable where he kept a fresh mount.

They were running!

Topping-out on one of the lower peaks of the Big Range, Sheriff Casey McCall lifted his hat, blotted sweat from his brow with his shirtsleeve, and squinted down into the glare of the flats below where the two riders were clearly heading for the Gauntlets.

He swore. He didn't know this part of the Gauntlets all that well. Most men avoided it. Rough as a shucked cob, full of sudden drop-offs and dead-end trails. Plus some mighty fine spots if a man had notions to set up an ambush.

He didn't think Rainey and Murphy would be that

stupid, but, well, they were killers and by now they must've figured he was after them to ask more probing questions about just *how* Cleve O'Day came to have so many bullets in him.

But there was a solution, and one he didn't hesitate to put into action.

This was Buck Buckley's stamping ground. Butting-up against his nor'-west pastures, he had chased straying cows in here many a time and knew it like the back of his hand.

Most likely Rainey and Murphy were going to cut across the lower west corner, far away from Buck's spread, but the lawman knew this area well enough to find a pass that Buck had shown him one time when he was on the trail of a bully who called himself 'Rockfist', and who had gone too far trying to prove it by beating a man half to death. He was now known as 'Lefty', because his so-called 'rockfist' was no longer any use to him, and both knees had somehow been crippled: injuries very similar to those he had inflicted upon his luckless victim.

In ten minutes, McCall realized now he hadn't taken as much notice of the landmarks as he should have when Buckley had led him through here. Impatient to nail the bully, he had followed Buckley more than watching for landmarks for some future use – *like now, dammit!*

But he did see the trail over the timbered rise that led to Buckley's place. He touched his spurs quickly to his mount's sweating flanks.

*

He was impatient to get there, and Buckley didn't waste any time after McCall told him why he needed his help.

'Be best if I come with you instead of tryin' to explain where to go; be quicker,' the rancher said, already hurrying towards the corrals where one of his few cowhands was setting a leaning post more firmly in the hard ground.

'Sam! Saddle my bay! Pronto!'

Sam Hall detected the urgency as well as seeing the edgy sheriff. He gave a short wave and climbed through the rails, reaching down a rope from a corner post.

Buckley jogged towards the bunkhouse and, by the time he came back, wearing his six-gun and carrying a rifle and filled water canteen, his mount was waiting, stomping a forefoot and giving a short whinny of greeting as Sam Hall finished tightening the cinchstrap.

'Buy you a drink next time we go to town,' Buckley promised the cowhand as he slid his rifle into the saddle scabbard and swiftly climbed aboard the bay.

Sam grinned and licked his lips elaborately as he waved the two riders off.

Buckley led the lawman towards the hazy hills of this part of the mountains, McCall hesitating a little.

'This the quickest way?' he called.

'If they're going to cross – and from what you said, I reckon they'll make for Storm Canyon if they aim to hide out.'

'They will! They know I didn't believe their story

77

about you shootin' Cleve so many times.' Then he frowned. 'They'll be in sight of the Munro place, too. Hope they don't try anythin'. Think there's only the woman there now since the kid brother moved out.' He sounded a mite concerned, like the good lawman he was.

'Want to stop by and check?'

McCall thought for a moment then shook his head. 'No. I reckon Rainey and Murph're are in too much of a hurry to detour across two cricks and – well, I can't see any reason why they'd want to delay.'

He had to spur his already sweating horse to catch up with Buckley who was now riding in amongst the brush on the lower slopes.

Crashing his mount through some of the bushes, McCall yelled, 'They wouldn't come this way! This'll take 'em straight down to the stage-station and—'

'If they kept goin' and rounded that leaning bluff it would, but there's a cleft this side that leads above the stage-station and down the other side to the river.'

McCall frowned. 'Yeah, you know that because you live out here, but would Rainey and Murphy?'

'They tried their luck tossing a wideloop over my cattle one time, not long ago; drove 'em over the river ford tryin' to cover their tracks, so they'll know about it all right. I caught up with 'em just after they got this far.'

McCall stiffened, staring at the deadpan rancher.

'Damn me! So *that's* what happened to them two that time they showed up beat-up all to hell, could hardly walk, staggered into town on foot, wouldn't say what had happened to 'em! You caught 'em rustlin' your cows and taught 'em a lesson!'

Buckley shrugged. 'Quicker an' better'n waitin' to put 'em through the courts where they could mebbe get off by hiring a sharp lawyer like Rainey's brother-in-law.'

McCall's mouth was tight as he looked at Buckley with narrowed eyes. 'Yeah, I forgot about that two-faced twister! But I'm not s'posed to hear any of this ... wild stuff, Buck!' Then added, 'Damn your hide!'

Buck merely gave a brief salute and kept riding.

McCall watched for a moment or two, then shook his head and followed. 'Goddamn vigilante!' he declared, without rancour.

Maybe so, he added silently to himself a few seconds later. *But it sure got the job done ... legal or not.*

'We do it by the book this time, Buck!' he said aloud and with authority. 'By – the – book!'

Buckley gave no sign that he had heard ... and the sheriff swore, spurring his mount on.

Casey McCall had been wrong about one thing: Rainey and Murphy *were* desperate and stupid enough to try an ambush. It was dangerous, mighty hazardous country so they just might be able to pull it off and get clear afterward. *Might....*

Buckley had been here only once before, chasing a big, gleaming black mustang he had wanted for a stud horse.

In fact, it damn near killed him because the edge of a precarious trail had crumbled and both he and his mount had taken a tumble that started a small avalanche.

He had been lucky to get out of it with a broken arm – the left one – and a couple of dozen cuts and bruises. His horse had not been so lucky – both forelegs broken – so Buck had had to shoot it.

He never did catch that black mustang, either.

He hipped in the saddle now to call a warning to the sheriff, and that was when Murphy and Rainey opened up.

But the pursuers were some distance apart and while a concentrated volley might have been enough to stop them if they'd been closer together, this time it failed. Though not a *complete* failure, because McCall's horse was shot out from under him and he took a heavy fall.

But Casey McCall had a reputation for being physically tough and, with blood flooding down one side of his face, he rolled with the sliding gravel and squirmed behind a low rock. It must have surprised the hell out of Rainey and Murphy when he raked their position – marked by the gunsmoke rising from their rifles – emptying his six-gun, the lead humming and whining about their ears.

McCall rolled onto his side to reload but the blood from his head wound hampered him, blinding him on that side, and he fumbled badly, spilling cartridges.

Even above the hammering of his own six-gun

Buckley heard the lawman's explicitly descriptive curses.

He emptied the Colt, saw his horse was too far off for him to dive for the saddle scabbard and get his rifle. Then, as he gathered himself, Murphy and Rainey dropped out of sight over their ridge and within seconds he heard them riding off. There was nothing to do now but start back riding double. McCall was closer to the horse so Buck gestured to him impatiently to climb into the saddle while he reloaded.

'Sons of bitches!' roared McCall as he finally got his Colt reloaded, holstered it and ran for Buck's mount.

His words echoed around the rocks but they both knew they had lost their quarry ... for now, anyway.

Still, Buckley hesitated before climbing up behind the sheriff, now with a rough kerchief bandage on his head.

'Case, make for that wall of yellow rock.'

The sheriff twisted so quickly he heard his neck creak and let loose with still more curses before he said, 'We gonna fly? 'Cause that's the only way we'll get over that!'

Buck gave him a brief smile, little more than a twitching of one side of his mouth. 'Care to bet?'

'Ah, you can't climb it, for hell's sake!'

'Ride closer. Come on, McCall! Move!'

Reluctantly, and with bad grace, the lawman rode closer to the wall. He could see small shadows here and there, marking hollows on the rockface, but—

'There're barely any handholds! One slip if you're

near the top – and I say *if* – I'll be scraping you up with my Bowie knife! Hey! What the hell!'

He felt hands grip his shoulders briefly, then he was rocked in the saddle as weight was suddenly transferred from behind him on the horse and—

The man he knew as Buck Buckley was on the wall – spread-eagled against its face, fingers and toes feeling for – and finding! – enough purchase to drive him upwards – up – up the vertical face of the wall. And fast…!

And suddenly McCall felt his belly lurch.

'Jesus Christ!' he breathed, but there was a good deal of reverence in the expression just the same. 'Now I know you! Wade Craddock, the Human Fly!'

Halfway up the wall, Buck paused, but didn't look down. Instead, he started across the face of the obstruction.

'*Wrong*, Case. Name's *not* Wade Craddock.'

'The hell it ain't!' There was confidence now in the sheriff's voice. 'You were with Hanlon Montague's Show of Heroes! One of his top attractions. He even put up fifty bucks for anyone who could come up with a vertical wall you couldn't scale!'

McCall said it like a punctuation: a few years ago, it was the name of one of the biggest travelling circuses in the West … famous throughout the entire country, drawing crowds like ants to honey.

Buck looked down over one shoulder. 'Leave it, Case. Name's *not* Wade Craddock!' It was a flat denial, said with feeling.

'Ah! Quit stallin'! You were bearded in those days, talked kinda funny. You was supposed to have some sort of foreign accent – for your act, I guess – but you're Wade Craddock, all right. Bet my life on it.'

Buck continued to stare down. 'Don't be rash, Case, you could end up dead.'

'The hell with you! I know who you are, but why you're denyin' it beats me. You were a top star, nothin' to be ashamed of....' His voice began to slow and drop in volume. 'No, wait! Hell, there was some trouble, right? Your name was all over the West because— *Damn*! Sorry I brought it up. I can respect you not wantin' to talk about it, but why deny your name now? It was a long time ago and—'

'You're not the only one who remembers, Case.'

The sheriff frowned, then his gaze quickened. 'No-oo, I guess not. The kid's father set some wolves on your trail, as I recollect—' It was obvious McCall expected an answer.

'There's still some out there – lookin'. Hopin' that damn big bounty can still be collected.'

'Hell almighty! So that's why you cussed a blue streak when they put that picture of you in the *Gazette*! It told 'em where you were! Why, must be five years ago—'

'Seems a helluva lot longer'n that. He swore he'd never stop hunting me down. Has the money to back him too. Even sold one of his *ranchos* to finance it.'

'Unforgiving sonuver, ain't he? Mex or somethin'.'

'One of the old-style Spanish nobility, I guess you'd

call 'em. All full of what they see as "honour" and "revenge". Never give up till they're satisfied they've avenged the death of one of the family.'

'An' there I was, shoutin' your name all over the damn countryside.'

'Not quite my name, Casey. It's "Wayne", not "Wade".'

McCall looked at him steadily. 'No. It's Buck Buckley as far as I'm concerned, and to anyone else who happens to ask.'

Buck nodded. 'Good of you, Case.' He glanced up at the wall rising above. 'Guess it don't matter whether I climb this or not now. Thought it'd be a shortcut and I could pick 'em off from up there, but they'll be long gone by now.'

McCall sighed, mouth tight. 'I'll send off a few tele-graphs when we get back. Know some of the lawmen in them Sweetwater towns up where they're headed. Couple might be good enough to throw a loop over 'em.'

'Rather they shot 'em down.' McCall tensed and Buck added quietly, 'Rainey knows me from way back. He gets a whiff of reward money and I'm gonna have to start carryin' a mirror.'

As he saw McCall's puzzled frown, he added quietly, 'So I can watch my back.'

CHAPTER 7

DEADLY
PIGGY-BACK

McCall said there was no way he was going to climb the goddamned cliff and that Buckley should go on to the top and report what he could see from there.

'You've got the experience.'

It made sense, though Buck would have preferred not to have to make the full climb.

'Y-eahh – OK. You get ready to ride round the base, mebbe we can cut the sonuvers off or something.'

'Here, take my carbine. Slip it through the back of your belt, be easier than trying to manhandle your rifle.'

Buckley agreed, slid the weapon through his belt at his back, and started his human fly act – this time unpaid and with an audience of only one.

But he hadn't climbed more than a few feet when it all came back to him, rushing from out of the past.

The horror he'd lived with for – what? – five years now? Five long, long years....

And it had all started with laughter and thrills in Happy Hanlon Donahue's 'Show'.

It was really a circus but Hanlon Donahue preferred to call it 'The Show' – more prestige he reckoned. Hanlon was a bit of a snob but a generous character: he arranged his show for a Colorado town called Rafter's Crossing, struggling to get back on its feet after an unseasonal flood. He donated some of his takings to help the town's recovery.

The venue was at the foot of a ridge named Candyrock – a formidable, vertical slab of granite with barely a handhold on its smooth face.

Buckley, then known as Wayne Craddock, the Human Fly, doubted if even he could find enough handholds. But he had a reputation to live up to and not only did he manage to make his climb a shade faster than normal, but Hanlon decided to cash in on the audience's excitement by offering free tickets to the next performance plus fifty dollars to anyone who would ride on Craddock's shoulders during his current climb.

'You're crazy!' Craddock had told Hanlon after his announcement. 'That wall's been practically swept clean of any handholds in the floods. Man, my fingers are bent outa shape already! They're bleeding – and you want to double-up on the performance?' He shook his head. 'Can't do it, Hanlon. *Won't*, if you prefer.'

But it was too late to withdraw the challenge after it had been made and, against his better judgement, he succumbed to Hanlon's fast talking and persuasion. Craddock finally agreed *but* only if his 'rider' was restricted to boys no older than their teens.

They couldn't argue very long about it – the audience was waiting for the first volunteer – so Hanlon agreed, and before the announcement's echoes had died, a line was already forming – kids fighting their parents as they wanted to take on the challenge, some angry when jealous schoolmates who had already joined the line called insults.

'I thought that was a yaller shirt you're wearin', Johnno, but it's only your back showin' through!'

'Hey, Kenny! You sit in somethin' wet—? Your pants are stickin' to you—! Not sure what with!'

'Monty! Stop your knees knockin'! Can't hear what the man's sayin'!'

This kind of thing stirred up a lot of yelling and catcalls and in the midst of it a tall, slim man in rich-looking Spanish clothes carried a boy about seven or eight to the fore, on his shoulders.

'Señor! You need look nor further!' He shook the worried looking boy as he held him up a little higher, the child struggling, barely suppressing tears. 'I am Capitano Miguel Tejerizo, from Hacienda Espuela.' He bent one leg, touching a big-wheeled spur on his ornate boots. 'The Spur, eh? My son, Michaelo, desires to accept your challenge! Tell him, my *pequeno amigo*!' He gave the wide-eyed child a shake. 'Tell him, my leetle frien'!' He lowered his voice. 'You will bring pride and honour to the name of Tejerizo!'

A squeaky, 'Si, señor, I-I accept …' could barely be heard.

Hanlon felt his arm grabbed in a painful vice and looked into Craddock's angry face as the man shook his head violently. 'Don't accept, Han! Hell, the kid's already wet himself! He'll claw my eyes out, or upset my balance on the wall. It was stupid callin' for kids in the first place!'

'The hell you callin' "stupid"!' growled Hanlon. 'Er – Señor Capitano, we accept your Little Mickey as the first to ride on the back of Wayne – *The* Human Fly!' He shouted the last, indicating Craddock with a sweep of his hand.

There was lots of cheering – and a heated argument between Craddock and Hanlon, that resulted in Craddock finally agreeing to carry the scared-looking Michael – Little Mickey – up the chosen wall on his back.

Of course, it all went wrong.

The child panicked, almost choked and blinded Craddock who reached up to prise the surprisingly strong little fingers out of his eyes. 'Come on, boy! It'll be all right.'

They were almost to the top when the boy's grip suddenly broke – and he fell. Craddock barely managed to keep from following him, swinging by his bleeding fingertips. He grabbed at the child as he plunged past … and missed.

The boy landed on the back of his neck and the crack was heard even above all the shouting and screams of the audience.

The tragedy was enough to lower a cloud of gloom over The Show. Craddock, a tough man, nonetheless threw up several times behind the tent, so upset was he.

But there was more to come … much more.

Capitano Tejerizo was not only a powerful man, but an unnaturally devoted father: he had poured all his affection and hopes, bordering on obsession, on Little Mickey, his only son.

One of the first things he did after the child's death, was to bankrupt Hanlon Donahue, by vicious pressure applied to the showman's backers, and only just failed in an attempt to have Donahue charged with 'culpable negligence'. Then he learned his wife could give him no more children!

He was like a madman, going after every employee of Hanlon's, messing up their lives in some way, simply because they worked for Hanlon. But he sent *killers* after Craddock.

The first assassin used a knife and Wayne Craddock had a real fight on his hands. He was jumped in the dark near where he had a room – and there turned out to be two of them. The second man waited in deep shadow and Craddock unwittingly played into the killers' hands by dodging and weaving, not realizing that his every move had been anticipated already by these professionals. The second man lunged out of the shadows and his knife sliced across Craddock's ribs.

Feeling the hot blood flow he instinctively clamped his arm down on the killer's, pinning it firmly as the man tried to turn the knife for a deeper thrust. Craddock smashed his forehead across the killer's nose and heard it splinter an instant before the man screamed. It was a womanish scream and stopped him in his tracks. Which was just as well, for the other assailant lunged with *his* knife and it sank to the hilt – but in his companion as Craddock stepped aside nimbly.

'Dio mio!' the man cried in alarm and Craddock spun him around, smashed him face first into the wall, spun him again, and kneed him in the groin, jumping clear.

There were others waiting to come after him and he drew his gun, coldly shot two ... the rest scattered.

Bleeding, he escaped ... but with Spanish threats ringing in his ears. He allowed that was normal enough, seeing what had happened. He ran until he was deep in the shadow of the rock wall, feeling desperately for fingertip and toeholds, as he climbed faster than he ever had before. A gun thundered below and bullets whined past his ears.

'You are a dead man, Señor!' the capitano's voice threatened, spittle flying. 'For the rest of your life – which I swear on my child's blood will not be long! – I will hunt you down, you and your family – every single one! I will wipe your name from the face of the earth forever!'

Craddock savvied the rage of the capitano, knew he

would need to quit this part of the country for good
– likely the powerful Spaniard's rage would die away
slowly – never forgotten completely, of course, but time
would reduce it to a mere simmering level rather than
the raging, hot-blooded madness El Capitano was
feeling right now. But perhaps the colder rage would
be even worse.

As time passed, he learned that Capitano Tejerizo
was a very powerful man who had many enemies. The
man had convinced himself that the death of Little
Mickey had been deliberately planned as revenge by his
enemies for blood debts owed from his past. Craddock,
of course, he believed had been the instrument used to
administer this shocking form of revenge, so would pay
for it with his own blood!

The capitano immediately sold some of his land and
put up 50,000 pesos as a bounty on Craddock's head:
literally it would be paid to any man who brought him
the actual head of Wayne Craddock.

So far, no one had come even close to collecting.

But life was not easy these days, Craddock allowed:
looking over his shoulder all the time, leery of everyone
he passed on the street, walking wide of dark or even
dim areas, entering any room he rented by tedious but
essentially cautious means – and losing sleep! Lots of
lost sleep.

Hell, yes! He had to admit that once or twice he had
dozed over an evening meal in some café or saloon, he
was so damn tired, snapping awake violently, frighten-
ing his fellow diners as he brought up his cocked Colt,

looking around wildly, before a modicum of sanity
returned.

And, of course, riding his range – even after five
years – was one of constant, never-ending vigilance. He
was worried that some day he might be jumpy enough
to shoot a friend he was slow to recognize.

The Human Fly!

Hell! There were times lately when he even hoped
that someone would swat him and end all the stress,
or at least, come out into the open to give him a target
he could shoot at instead of *him* being the target …
constantly.

He let his hair grow to shoulder-length, gave up
shaving to allow his beard to flourish. He tried a false
accent, changed his name a few times, but once or
twice forgot what he was calling himself and, although
it caused some trouble and a lot of off-the-cuff suspi-
cion, he had managed to get by.

That damn Spanish ranchero! He was not only much
more powerful than anyone had thought, he was much
more mean with it. Totally unforgiving, he would
never even listen to any explanation, never agree to
a meeting. It was amazing that their paths had never
crossed in those five long years – or maybe they had,
sometime, without either knowing it.

But somehow – by a hunch, intuition, call it what
you will – Buck Buckley *knew* that the inevitable confrontation was coming and it might as well be soon.

Well, let's get it over with, he thought, almost
eagerly. The constant threat of death by an unknown

assassin was a burden he could do without.

But he didn't know about the other danger that faced him.

Yet....

He was out of practice at climbing, though he knew the movements would come in their order, subconsciously.

With McCall waiting impatiently below, muscles he had forgotten he had aching and screaming, he made his way up at a steep angle, gaspingly remembered at last to level this off more, even though it meant exposing himself for longer on the face of the wall.

Also, for his act with Hanlon Donahue, he had used specially made boots. Although they looked like an ordinary pair of riding boots, the leather was much softer and pliable on the uppers, the toe part of the sole was patterned with a series of ridged grips that allowed him to seem suspended, yet still look as if he was hanging by his fingernails – literally. It might be too much to say that these boots made the chore easier, but the fact was they did.

And he wished like hell that he had them on now.

Sweat blinded him; his breath heaved out in slow half-choking gasps, and his arms – well, he sure hoped he wouldn't have to try to shoot it out with Rainey or Murphy until he was down on flat, solid ground.

But finally, he heaved over the rim with a series of rasping gasps, rolled onto his back, forgetting for the moment the carbine. He cursed as the metal parts dug into him, swiftly twisted onto one side and worked the weapon free of his belt, then lay there, chest heaving, limbs like throbbing bars of iron, heart beating so hard he thought it must surely crack a rib or two.

The sun blasted down on his congested face and he closed his eyes against its glare. But his eyelids glowed red and he turned his head painfully to the side, raised one screaming arm enough to cast a shadow over his upper face.

From a long way off, he heard McCall's voice.

'Damn hoss stepped in a rabbit hole, Buck! Nothin' broke but I can't ride him – you're on your own now.'

Buckley didn't have enough breath to curse aloud but the suitable words raged around inside his over-heated brain.

'Just – what – I – needed!' he told himself.

And then he heard the clatter of hoofs, below and to his left.

Sweeping his hat back so it hung around his throat on the tie-thong, he eased to the very edge, looking over cautiously.

There they were!

No mistaking those two, and they were smart enough to know that with his ability to scale seemingly unclimbable walls he might well be above them. They scanned the wall rims, Rainey to the left, Murphy to his right.

Buck lay very still, knowing the slightest movement against the skyline would draw their gazes, glad his hat was hanging down between his shoulders.

For one tense moment he thought Rainey had locked his gaze on his position – but the man turned to Murphy, speaking briefly.

Their horses were gleaming with sweat and Murphy's seemed to favour its left shoulder. As he watched, the rider leaned forward and rubbed the area briskly but the mount started acting up and, instead of trying to soothe its pain, Murph bad-temperedly cuffed it hard across the ear. The horse jerked its head in annoyance and swivelled it so it could bite Murphy's leg.

Apparently it was on target, or nearly so, and Murph rose quickly in the stirrups swearing plenty loud enough for Buck to make out the words.

'Keep it down!' yelled Rainey – just as loud – without realizing he was only adding to the din. 'I'll keep this knotheaded crowbait down!'

Murphy lashed with his quirt and the horse whinnied and spun, bucking violently, Murphy almost toppling from the saddle. Rainey, with a look of exasperation, rammed his mount into the other. It shrilled and staggered and Murphy slid part way off, snatched at the bridle, kicking his boots free of the stirrups, falling the rest of the way.

There was a good deal of dust and a lot of cussing, but Rainey leaned from his saddle and grabbed the other animal's flying reins, yanking it to a snorting standstill.

'Well, if Craddock's within a goddamn mile of here he knows where we are after that!' he snapped angrily.

Murphy was still beating at his horse in anger until Rainey leaned down and knocked the man's hat off his head with his six-gun barrel.

Murph staggered and grabbed at his head, which was bleeding from the Colt's foresight. 'The hell you do that for?'

'Use your head or I'll knock it clean off your shoulders!' Rainey snarled. 'An' quit beatin' up on your hoss! I've told you before it's stupid hatin' an animal you might have to depend on to save your neck.'

'Aaaaah – can't stand the bastard gettin' the better of me. Next time ... Judas Priest! *There he is!*'

Murphy had glanced up at the precise moment Buck's hat caught on a rock and pulled him back and down with a jerk as he moved away from the edge, the tie-thong tightening around his throat.

Murphy dropped to one knee in a blurred, fast movement, his Colt coming up, firing two rapid shots. Buck reared back as the bullets chewed gravel and kicked it into his face. *Damn good shooting!* he allowed as he sprawled, almost losing his grip on the carbine.

By the time he had rolled onto his belly, levered a shell into the breech and heaved forward, using his elbows, Murphy and Rainey were moving – in opposite directions: old hands at this kind of confrontation.

Buck fired three fast shots, the flat sound of the short-barrelled carbine slapping at his ears, as he swung the muzzle on first one target, then the other.

He made a hit!

It was Rainey, and the bullet seared him above

the right ear, slamming his head around as his body staggered and followed that direction. He stumbled, put down a hand to keep him from falling all the way and, as he fell, twisted enough to get his six-gun free of leather.

Buck had jumped up as they put distance between them and the wall. The carbine whipped to his shoulder and just as he triggered, Murphy fired his rifle in a short, vicious burst. By luck or design the three bullets hit the edge almost directly beneath Buck's feet. The dry earth crumbled and he staggered as he lost his footing. The carbine fell, turning over and over, bouncing off protruding rocks as it clattered to ground level. He twisted violently, looking for something to grab so as to keep from following the gun. His lower body slipped over the edge and he grabbed at a shaggy bush growing right on the lip – which was his undoing. The roots were shallow and while he got a good grip on the bush itself, the weight of his sliding body yanked hard enough to pull him up with a jerk, but only for a moment before the roots tore free in a burst of dust and gravel.

This side of the wall was – luckily for him – not nearly as vertical as the side he had climbed. But it was steep and he hit hard, slid and somersaulted and rolled all the way to the bottom.

By that time he was dazed from his head hitting a rock that split the skin above his left eye. The blood flowed as, instinctively, he reached for the wound and then the breath was beaten from him as his body jarred to a stop at the bottom.

Dazed, vision blurred, he started to sit up groggily – a boot caught him on the side of the jaw, and stretched him out, barely conscious.

'Well, howdy, Craddock!' said Rainey, leaning down and slamming his Colt's barrel against Buck's throbbing head as he cocked the hammer. 'Good to meet you at close quarters! You son of a bitch!' He swung the Colt again.

Viciously.

CHAPTER 8

'I WANT YOU TO DIE!'

It was a world he wanted to leave as quickly as possible.

Cold, dark, uncomfortable – lightning bolts of pain shooting through his aching body. He groaned and lifted an arm that felt like he was holding a sack of bolts as he felt for the source of the throbbing in his head.

He touched a wet, sticky place on his left temple, knew it was blood. And then his hand was roughly yanked away and a voice rasped, as if coming from a long way off.

'Comin' round now.'

His aching brain vaguely recognized it and by the time a second voice answered he had remembered. Rainy and Murphy. It was the latter who had spoken first.

'You coulda killed him!' growled Rainey.

'Well, what's it matter? We're gonna do it anyway.' A

hand slapped Buck's face brutally, once, twice, a third time.

'Hear that, Craddock? We're – gonna – kill – you. Just have to make up our minds whether to do it before we cut off your head, or let you feel it happenin'.'

'Come on, Murph! Christ, it's bad enough having to take his head to that mad Spaniard without prolongin' it!'

'Mebbe. Shoot him now and I'll take a walk while you do the rest.'

Murphy snorted derisively. 'By hell, you are squeamish, ain't you?'

'I'll shoot him if you like, but – not the other.'

'Ah, go take a walk then. I'll do the lot. Just remember we won't get no fifty thousand bounty if we don't! That capitano's crazy all right, but he's r-i-c-h! An' he wants to make sure this sonuver's dead before he pays up.'

'Well, long as he does pay, I s'pose. What the—'

They had been crouched one either side of the battered Buckley and suddenly his right leg shot out, the boot catching Murphy in the neck, knocking him sprawling into Rainey who was just starting to rise – and nicely off balance so that both killers went down in a tangle.

One of the guns exploded but Buck didn't take time to see whose it was – and didn't care. As long as he could get under cover of one of those rocks just a few yards away.

His legs were weak, barely under his control, and

he weaved, stumbled to hands and knees, moving awkwardly but still in the direction of the rocks. He was vaguely aware of the killers untangling themselves, saw Rainey struggling for a dropped pistol and then he dived over the first low rock.

A gun hammered three fast shots and bullets whined as they ricocheted. He ducked and then sprawled full length, rolling, but finding the space too cramped so that he banged a knee and pain writhed through his leg. Staying on his belly, fingers clawing into the coarse sand, he grunted aloud as he heaved through a narrow space between two boulders.

The guns blazed and he winced as the bullets snarled and spray of rock chips stung his face.

There was cursing behind him and he almost managed a grin: those two fools had panicked when he had surprised them and taken off, shooting wild – not counting their shots!

Now they had to stop and reload.

Not that it was much of an advantage for him, because he was groggy and disorientated, but, thankful for small mercies, he thought as he skidded and fell, then crawled a few feet before clawing his way upright.

'There!' one of them shouted. Three shots hammered and he abruptly found himself flat on his belly.

But there was room to crawl down here!

Most of the rocks seemed to be touching each other, but were of such irregular shapes that there were small spaces of various sizes at ground level. Head spinning, feeling like a herd of longhorns had passed over him, Buck squirmed and wriggled through these tight spaces as the killers searched where he had last gone to ground.

'He must be half snake to get through here!' Murphy snarled and Buck knew they had discovered the random spaces at ground level.

But he kept going, hearing occasional curses that slowly faded, and realized he was gaining on them.

There was a period of quiet that had him feeling more confident of making a getaway, and then a voice called – ahead of him!

'There's a clearin' here! The only one. We've got him, Murph! He has to come out this way!'

'Then finish the sonuver as soon as you see him!'

'Be a pleasure!'

Heart pounding, lungs straining for more air, Buck lay there under a rock, muscles screaming, afraid to move because he would have to twist and turn to get out into that damn clearing Rainey had found.

He couldn't move his head enough to see if there was any other way, but instinctively he knew there wasn't: it seemed they had him, literally, between a rock and that proverbial hard place.

Then Rainey yelled and crashed off his rock at the same time as Buck heard a rifle whiplash at an angle to the left, where he had seen thick brush.

'Rainey?' called Murphy, edgy concern in the word. 'What…?'

Then the rifle cracked again and again and Rainey yelled, 'Someone in the brush! He can pin us down here, goddammit!'

'Not me! You stay if you want!'

Murphy's Colt hammered a couple of shots and the rifle answered, bringing more curses from the killers.

'C'mon, Murph! Forget him for now!'

'*Just* for now, goddammit!' Murphy yelled as his six-gun's hammer fell on an empty chamber. 'Let's get the hell outa here!'

Not believing his ears, Buck lay very still, hearing all the sounds that indicated Murph and Rainey were jumping and clambering over the boulders, making a run for it.

The rifle fired several more times – to hurry them along, he figured – and then came the whinny of star-tled mounts as they were raked by urgent spurs.

Rapid hoofbeats followed and swiftly faded, along with the dying echoes of the gunfire.

Buck, heart pounding, hoping he had interpreted the sounds of getaway correctly, cautiously squirmed out of the rocks and looked around him before climb-ing into the clearing.

He froze as he saw movement at the edge of the trees and brush. Sunlight glinted on a rifle barrel and he tensed as it swung in his direction.

'Just stay right where you are!'

He blinked and stopped dead; *it was a woman's voice*!

'And don't think for one moment that your troubles are over, Buckley, or whatever you call yourself now! Because I want to see you die! And I'm going to kill you in a few minutes.'

Her words froze him, but he did as she ordered, though he holstered his six-gun before lifting his hands shoulder high.

She stepped out of the trees, a tallish woman in checkered shirt with a cowhide vest over it, denim work trousers and scuffed riding boots. He couldn't see her face very well because she had the rifle raised and was looking along the barrel. She wore a narrow-brimmed, buff-coloured hat with a snakeskin band.

She walked slowly, carefully picking a way over tree roots and loose stones on the ground. She didn't stop until she was only about six feet from him.

'Well, you can't miss from there,' he told her.

'And I won't … when I'm ready.'

She lowered the rifle to waist level and he saw she had a round face, suntanned, with penetrating dark eyes as she studied him. Light-brown hair came just level with her shoulders and seemed to have a natural wave or curl.

She looked feminine enough, but the familiar way she held that rifle and regarded him with that cold stare made him tighten up.

Then he looked at her face more closely, with the tight mouth and small nose, and he felt that warning lurch in his belly again: she clearly hated him, was eager to kill him.

'Wait a minute! I know you!'

Her expression didn't change. 'We've never met,' she said curtly.

'Mebbe not – properly. You're the one tried to shoot

me back in town *and* out on my range, aren't you?'

'I should've used my rifle. And you'd be already dead!'

'Well, why the hell...? What've you got against me?'

'You killed my brother! You damned murderer!'

'Now, hold up! I dunno who the hell you are, so sure dunno whether I knew your brother or not.'

'You just shot him down in cold blood!'

'Miss, I dunno what you're talkin' about. You'll have to give me more information.' He stopped abruptly, stared at her more intensely, watching the knuckle of her trigger finger. 'I-I thought I either knew you from somewhere, or had seen you before, but I never did get a clear look at you back at my ranch, and yet ... your face seems familiar. That ... roundness.' He paused again and then nodded. 'Wait! I remember now. No! I don't think I have seen you close enough to recognize, but I did see someone mighty like you.' His mouth went dry as he recalled entering the Grantland Bank, saw the moon-faced young robber German Jack called 'Loop' as he berated him for not locking the door. 'Your brother named Loop?'

She stiffened and for a moment he thought he was a dead man. But she eased the pressure on the rifle's trigger and, strangely, he thought he saw a glint in her eyes like – like tears...?

'German Jack called him "Loop",' he said gently, getting ready to dive for the ground.

She flinched slightly. 'His name was "Lew"!' she said emphatically.

He nodded slowly. 'Must've been Jack's accent – sounded to me like he said Loop.'

She gave him a sharp look and then slid her eyes away from his face.

'Your brother looks a lot like you, and he rode with Jack, didn't he.'

'What're you talking about? German Jack is an outlaw and….' Her voice trembled and he could read the anger at herself in her face. She stopped and took a deep breath. 'Yes! But Lew was very young, had romantic notions about life in the West. He thought riding with outlaws was exciting. He didn't seem to worry much about what they did – didn't try to profit by it – enjoyed the thrill. Breaking the law to him was – well, he saw it as some kind of adventure….'

Her voice faded as she tried to avoid crying.

'Lady, I savvy what you're saying, but Lew was still with a gang robbing the Grantland Bank. And he tried to kill me when I bought into it – I had to protect myself.'

'Six men killed in a matter of seconds! That seems more than "protection" to me!'

'Call it self-defence then,' he told her curtly. 'What did you expect me to do? Stand there and let them shoot me down?'

Her lips were almost bloodless now as she compressed them and her breasts heaved with emotion. He watched that rifle warily as tears rolled down her cheeks. 'He – he was just a boy! Not even eighteen years old!'

'Mebbe so, but he was riding with outlaws who'd killed before.' In a lower voice he added, 'I can savvy that he saw some sorta glamour in that. I rode with a wild bunch for a while when I was young and full of vinegar. Short stretch in jail straightened me out, though. Look, I'm sorry Lew got killed, but I had no choice.'

'You – you sound like a professional gunfighter to me! And if so, you have no right to tell me whether my brother was doing right or wrong.'

'Miss, be straight with yourself. If you *knew* Lew was breaking the law, why didn't you make him leave Jack's gang? Or at least try to talk him into doing it? You want to blame his death on somebody, well, mebbe you should look in the mirror.'

'Oh! Oh, you – you bastard! How dare you?'

She swayed uncertainly. Shuffled her feet to find balance and stumbled against a tree. He took three long, swift strides and snatched the rifle out of her hands. Startled, she gripped the tree now and stared at him with wet, wide eyes.

He held the rifle with the barrel pointing at the ground. 'Relax, I ain't gonna shoot you. I'm sorry I spoke so rough, but – well, you gotta admit you're all one-sided in this. You're not being honest with yourself about Lew. He took his chances and he lost – like a lot of others. It's sad for you, I guess, but—'

'Don't you dare pretend you feel sorry for me! I-I mean, what sort of man can kill six men in six seconds! My God, that's – that's akin to out-and-out murder!'

He shook his head slowly. 'Lady, you can sure twist

things around. Look, I'm grateful to you for saving my neck and I'm truly sorry about Lew, but there's nothing either of us can do to change that. You gotta accept it.'

'Oh, go to hell, you murderer! I only "saved" you, as you call it, so I could kill you! I want to see you die! And – and I hope I have that pleasure!'

He nodded. 'Yeah, well, let's go our separate ways and neither of us'll have to worry about that. Where's your horse?'

'My horses are where you won't find them.'

'Then both of us've got long walks ahead – why you bring more than one horse?' He saw her face and then he smiled thinly. 'Oh, I get it, to carry my body away – right?'

'I absolutely hate you!'

'I'm gettin' that impression. But it oughtn't to take me long to find a couple of horses. Mebbe I'll leave you one.'

'I – I'll set the law on you for horse stealing. I'll tell them you violated me first, and I'll make it sound so – *vivid* – that they'll hang you!'

He gave her a bleak look. 'Well, you hate hard, I'll give you that. On second thoughts, I'll take both mounts with me. A walk in the fresh air might help to clear your head.' He touched a hand to his hat brim and backed away.

'I won't have a home until I see you dead!'

She shouted this last as he left and, despite himself, he felt a tingle of goosebumps.

CHAPTER 9

AVENGER

By whistling short and sharp through his teeth, in the traditional cowboy way when calling his horse, he found the two mounts the girl had brought tethered in a grove of somewhat bedraggled cottonwoods – a grey and a chestnut. It was simple enough: he just followed the whinnies as the animals answered his whistles.

The grey was the only one with short stirrups and carrying saddlebags, which he searched swiftly.

He found a creased receipt and letter from a veterinary he had heard of and it told him she was Loretta Munro – a name he recalled McCall mentioning briefly. She owned the Lazy M ranch at the twin forks of the river, north of his own spread and in more friendly-type country.

There wasn't much more he learned from the bag's contents: a few clean clothes, some hardtack carefully wrapped in waxed paper, a handful of small coins of various denominations, a pair of spurs without rowels and – most surprising – a used, short-stemmed corncob pipe with a chamois sack of tobacco and vestas.

Women smoking was not really acceptable but he didn't care one way or the other, so he strapped up the saddlebags and rode out, leading the grey horse.

He would probably leave it close to a stream or water hole where she would find it – after a considerable walk that would either calm her down, or make her more determined than ever to kill him.

'You're a mean sonuver, Buckley,' he told himself with a wry grin, as he rode away on the chestnut.

Life was becoming complicated: he had to watch out for Murphy and Rainey, men who would do their damnedest to kill him for a chance at the big reward offered by that loco Spanish ranchero. And now the girl: the longer she thought about making him pay for her brother's death – right or wrong – the more determined she would be to settle the score.

And from what he had seen and been able to judge, she might just turn out to be the most dangerous of them all.

Walking was not one of Loretta's favourite pastimes and she swore silently about the riding boots she was wearing. These boots were definitely not up to walking! she decided, but there was no choice.

The ground was rough and there were miles to cover yet before she could get within sight of home unless – unless he relented and did leave her a horse.

No! she decided. He's too mean for that!

But she would walk to the gates of Hell itself if it meant she would be able to reach him again and square things for Lew.

The thought died abruptly.

She'd heard the whinny of a horse ahead and just over that rise! Could it be he'd left her a mount after all, or had one gotten away and was finding its way home?

Stumbling, praying silently, she made her erratic way up the slope, pausing twice, gasping for breath, actually crawled the last few yards. Sweat stung her eyes and her hat fell forward. As she pushed it back from her eyes, she definitely heard the sounds of a horse only yards away.

No! Her heart suddenly hammered. Not *a* horse, more than one.

Blinking she wiped her eyes clear and her heart pounded as she saw two men with the grey mount she had tethered along with the chestnut earlier ... but there was no sign of the second animal.

They were chasing the grey, one man swinging a rope, throwing it expertly and settling the noose over its head. He drew it cruelly tight, skidding his own mount and jumping it around so that the rope became taut as a fiddle string, half-choking the grey and bringing it to its knees.

The second man rode in and deftly dropped a noose over its head also and they pulled the half-choked animal onto its side. As it kicked, Loretta jumped up, outraged.

'What the hell d'you think you're doing!' she cried.

They heard her and it was Rainey who saw her first. A tight grin split his hard, dusty face.

As he eased up the tension on his rope and allowed the horse to struggle to its feet, he said, 'Hey, Murph! We got us somethin' else to play with here.'

Murphy had already seen her and was riding in. She turned from him in alarm, her heart choking up into her throat as she made to run back down her side of the slope. But Murphy had loosened his rope and pulled it free of the still wide-eyed whickering horse.

She had taken only about six steps when she felt the constricting noose drop over shoulders: then it was yanked hard, pulling her off her feet.

There was a short time of confusion when she was tugged this way and that as she frantically tried to free herself. But the rope was taut – obviously these were range men and knew what they were doing. Panting, hat knocked off now, she sat there, unable to move her arms above the elbows, glaring up at the grinning man.

Rainey had dismounted, was now standing over her, holding his rope taut. 'You'd be the Munro woman, I guess.' He waited, but she didn't reply, only glared. 'Ooooh! You see that, Murph? If looks could kill, you'd be figurin' out what to put on my headstone right now!'

'She's a heller, ain't she? Look at the way she's strugglin'! Hey, sweetie, don't wear yourself out, we got somethin' for you to do that needs a good bit of energy! So save some of it for us – right, Kel?'

Rainey's mean eyes were narrowed now and he worked hand over hand along the rope to where it bit into her upper body. He clicked his tongue and suddenly flung the noose off her. It surprised Murphy as much as it did Loretta and he looked sharply at Rainey.

'Don't worry, Mike, she ain't goin' nowhere – for a while.'

'Ye-ah. Sounds good but – what about Craddock?'

She looked from one to the other, tense.

'He'll keep a mite longer. We can't pass up the chance of a leetle fun.' He bent down and thrust his sweaty face close enough for her to smell his sour breath. 'Can we, sweetie?'

She spat in his face.

Murphy's jaw dropped. Rainey reeled, hand actually shaking as he wiped the spittle from his cheek. He studied his damp fingers.

'Ju-das Priest! That the first time anyone's done that!' He backhanded her across the face, knocking her onto her side. 'But don't think you're gonna get away with it, you bitch!'

He suddenly reached for her blouse, but she spun away and he only caught a small section of the front. Buttons popped and part of a bare shoulder showed. The fear flared in her eyes now, but her mouth tightened determinedly and Rainey suddenly grinned.

'That's what I like! A bit of spirit! Fight tooth an' nail, while I—'

'I-I'll pay you to-to kill the man you call Craddock!'

she said suddenly. A desperate sound….

They exchanged glances and Rainey's grin widened. 'You mean old Buck? 'Course you do! Now what would a nice gal like you want to kill a man for? And how much you offerin', anyways?'

He winked at Murphy and she said quite seriously, 'A-a thousand dollars.'

Rainey arched his eyebrows as he looked at Murphy. 'A thousand bucks, Murph!'

'Each?' Murph asked.

She blinked but said slowly, 'Well – yes! I suppose I could manage that.'

'Wow, Kel! A thousand each for killin' a snake like Craddock? We'll be rich!'

'Aw, not that rich,' Rainey said, playing along. 'I mean, what about El Capitano? He's offerin' a mite more.'

'Mmmm, just a mite, though!'

They grinned at each other and she frowned slightly but said, 'Well, maybe I could match this other offer…?'

'Could be,' Rainey said, winking at Murphy again on the side the girl could see. 'Let's see. He – El Capitano, I mean – he said, if we bring him Craddock's head….'

Her eyes widened and her mouth worked but no sound came: the horror she felt was plain on her flushed face. She shuddered despite herself. 'My God!'

'Yeah. Well, if we take the capitano Craddock's head, he'll pay us – how much was it, Mike?'

'Bit more'n a thousand, I think.'

'Yeah, it was. How much though? Fifty thousand about right?'

She blanched. Knew they were toying with her and that it didn't mean anything good. 'I couldn't manage that.'

'No? Well, what could you do to kinda make up the difference, huh?'

'Wh-what?'

Murphy suddenly snapped his fingers. 'Hey, I got me an idea! She's a – well, a "she", and you an' me are "he's", and we ain't had the company of a real "she" for – well, a long time. I'm not countin' the whores, of course.'

'Oh, my God!'

In a moment of true panic she managed to tear free of the last loop of rope, with the two men grinning as they watched her roll to hands and knees and start to scramble towards the crest of the rise.

'Hey! Don't run off now! Murphy yelled, lunging after her.

Rainey was laughing as he went the other way to cut her off and she sprawled, rolled onto her back, hands up in front of her face.

The men moved in—

Until a cold voice said, 'Get away from her, you slimy animals!'

They spun towards the sound, Murphy stumbling, he twisted so fast. Rainey crouched, hand poised above his gun butt.

Buck stood just this side of the crest of the rise, one leg higher than the other on the slope. He held his rifle pointed between the two men.

Obviously they had been working together for a long time, for, without any signal that he could see, they moved apart, forcing him to choose two targets now. But his gun followed Murphy – they figured he would concentrate on Rainey as he was ready to draw, but Buck was an old hand at such confrontations, too.

He triggered at Murphy, and the man brought up his six-gun, but suddenly spun and staggered, falling to his knees as the weapon dropped to the ground. He clasped at his bleeding arm, teeth bared as he gritted against the sudden pain.

'Aw! Goddlemighty!'

The girl gave a small cry and put a hand to her mouth, eyes swivelling to Buck.

'Move to your left, miss,' he said quietly, and she hesitated only a moment before obeying.

Murphy was swearing, sitting awkwardly now, bright blood oozing between his gripping fingers. He raised his eyes to Buck's hard face. 'You – son of a – bitch!'

Buck moved his gunbarrel slightly. 'Like me to smash up that gun arm for good? No? Then wrap you neckerchief around the wound – nice and tight. OK, hold it there – and shut up!'

Murphy's pain-filled eyes were both angry and alarmed as he tugged his bandanna tight, using his teeth, and awkwardly went to work on his arm.

Buck casually pointed the rifle in Rainey's direction. He didn't have to say anything: the man narrowed his eyes but lifted his hands shoulder high, his gaze mighty wary. The girl was doing her best to adjust her blouse as well as she could, face flushed now, flicking her gaze towards Buck. There was no gratitude showing, just a cold anger. 'You, of all people!'

He smiled thinly. 'Kinda squares things, don't it, me rescuin' you now? No need to thank me, just get yourself fixed up. You!' He snapped the word at Rainey. 'Give her your jacket.'

'Like hell!'

The rifle lowered to his knee level. 'You like the idea of crutches? Mebbe a wheelchair...?'

Rainey was alarmed, his face suddenly pale. He quickly lifted his hands shoulder high again.

'Give – her – your – jacket!'

Rainey obeyed, looking as he would explode with his simmering anger. He tossed the denim garment at the girl's feet. She picked it up without a word, turned her back and struggled into it. When she turned around again she was holding the edges of the jacket across her chest.

'Th-thank you!' she said hoarsely, reluctantly. Buck smiled at the effort she put into the simple words, knowing she hated saying them to him.

He turned away, giving his attention to Rainey and the miserable Murphy. His rifle barrel jerked briefly towards the crest.

'Crawl on over, gents.'

Both men stared at him incredulously.

'W-What you say?' stammered Murphy.

'Do it!'

Murphy glanced at the simmering Rainey who started to speak, but when Buck's rifle barrel lowered towards his knees, he dropped onto them, wincing, then awkwardly began to half crawl and shuffle towards the crest.

Rainey glared as Buck arched his eyebrows and lifted the rifle barrel towards the ridge crest. 'Shuck your gunbelts first, gents. Think I'd forgotten 'em?'

'*I* won't forget you, you—!' growled Rainey.

'Hey! No bad language in front of the lady! *Move!*'

Rainey got to his hands and knees and began crawling, muttering blasphemies as the gravel cut into his knees through his trousers.

In about five minutes both were over the ridge and Buck moved to the very crest and watched, rifle at the ready, as they slid and skidded their way down the other side.

'Should've made it a race.' He was surprised at the way the girl was glaring at him. 'Somethin' wrong?'

'It would be *you* who had to come to my rescue!'

'Aw, my pleasure!' he said, somewhat bitterly.

She flushed, murmuring, 'I-I am grateful.'

He grinned and that made her even more angry. 'You nearly choked then! Relax, you're OK now. Why don't you take a draw on your pipe?' he suggested. 'Help settle you down.'

Her mouth sagged open a little, and she looked embarrassed; then, with an effort, glared back at him defiantly. 'I don't use it very often.'

'If it helps, why not?' He jerked his head upslope

behind him. 'You'll find the grey wandering some-where near where you left him, I guess – I'm using the chestnut – if that's OK by you, of course.'

'You have my permission!' She almost spat the words, as if she had any real choice.

'Good of you. Oh, yeah. There was this, too, in one of the saddlebags.' He tossed something small that glittered briefly in the sun and the derringer landed at her feet. 'Not much of a weapon unless it's used at close range.'

She was trembling with her anger – her small, gloved fists, curling up. 'Just as I intended to! To be sure I wouldn't miss!'

'Well, that's the idea of any kinda gun, I guess. You be OK now?'

'Of course I will!' She picked up the gun, broke it open and he smiled thinly as she looked at him coldly. 'Just as I thought. Empty!'

'Yeah, not much good that way.' He fumbled in his shirt pocket and tossed some small item that glinted briefly in the sunlight. It landed off to one side and behind her.

'For next time – in case I'm not around.'

He turned and started back to the crest as she scrab-bled for the tiny cartridge.

'You wait up!' she called, and he turned towards her as she pushed the cartridge into the derringer's breech, snapped the weapon closed and lifted it in both hands.

'You're too far away. A derringer's meant to shoot across a poker table, or rammed into someone's ribs.

Why you want to shoot me, anyway?'

'You – you ask that when you haven't even tried to deny you killed Lew?'

'No use denyin' it. He and his pards were doin' their best to kill me – you know all this. Nothing's going to change it: killing me won't bring him back.'

The jacket had fallen open and he saw that her breasts were heaving with her emotion. Trying not to make it too obvious, he prepared himself to take a dive downhill if she was crazy enough to shoot that derringer, which really wasn't too far away to reach him.

'Oh!' Her voice was trembling and he saw the glint of tears as she fought with her own feelings. 'I-I was looking forward to sending you to Hell, but I-I suppose I should show some sort of gratitude.'

'No need.' He touched his hat brim, vaguely amused to see the way she tensed at the movement of his arm. 'Guess I'll just say *adios*.' He gestured to the derringer. 'Use it in good health.'

Then he turned and walked back over the crest, rifle in a ready-to-shoot position as he looked for signs of Rainey and Murphy. But they were nowhere in sight.

He glanced back before he dropped below the level of the crest. She was still standing there, the derringer at her side now.

He started down to the clump of trees where he's left the chestnut earlier, after he'd heard her screams. The sooner he cleared this neck of the woods, the better, he decided.

That way he might even get to live a little longer.

CHAPTER 10

DANGEROUS FAVOUR

Sheriff Casey McCall urged his mount upslope with his heels, then suddenly his right hand released his grip on the reins as he whipped it back to the butt of his holstered Colt.

He cocked his head to one side, patting the horse's sweating neck and shushing it to stop it grunting in the back of its throat. He was damn sure that was a gunshot he had heard. A fair way off, likely beyond the crest, on the far side of the mountain. Just a single shot.

He listened for other shots following but nothing happened and he admitted, curtly, to himself that he had no idea what it meant. Someone hunting? Could be. A good shot, taking his quarry first time, but—

'Why the hell would anyone be hunting up there?'

Not likely to be a deer. Could be someone riding along and just spotted a wolf or some varmint.

'Quit it!' he growled. 'You've got no idea what it was an' the only way to find out is to go look.'

Then he saw something moving on the slopes up there. Two things – *men*! Crabbing their way carefully down the steep incline, one obviously favouring one arm.

He set the big black up at an angle, the horse snorting a protest, but obeying.

It hadn't taken him far before he recognized Murphy and Rainey. They saw him, Rainey picking up a short heavy branch lying a few feet away. Almost immediately he dropped it again after he apparently recognized the lawman. Both men stopped where they were, standing now.

'The hell you two doin'?' McCall asked, as he reined down. 'Where're your hosses?'

Sounding breathless, it was Rainey who answered, jerking a thumb up toward the top of the ridge.

'Up there.'

McCall's eyes pinched down. 'You gonna tell me or you think I'll play some stupid guessin' game with you?'

'Buckley made us crawl over the crest,' gasped Murphy. 'Lookit my arm! Sonuver shot me, threatened to blow off my knee caps, too.'

''S'right, Case,' Rainey said, mouth grim. 'I think he's gone loco or somethin'.'

'I'd guess the "or somethin'",' the sheriff said coldly.

'You two done somethin' to make Buckley take a gun to you. Now I ain't in no mood for games, so which one of you is gonna tell me exactly what happened?'

Murphy glanced at the grim-faced Rainey, but if he was looking for some sort of sign that would tell him how to act he was disappointed.

They could hardly say they'd come to kill Buck and take his head to the *capitano* so as to collect the massive reward, but they needed to say something.

'The girl,' Rainey said abruptly.

'What girl?' McCall asked slowly.

'The one runs that Lazy M spread up at Twin Forks,' said Murphy taking his cue from Rainey. 'Er – Munro, ain't it? Not a bad looker but sure has got a temper.'

'What about her?' McCall demanded through his teeth.

They realized he was in no mood for playing with words or anything else: he wanted straight answers, and he wanted them now. They respected him enough – as much as they could respect any lawman – to know not to push Casey McCall too far.

Murphy decided to let Rainey handle it and the look on that man's face warned him he would pay for throwing him to the wolves like this.

'Damn gal came outa nowhere, Case,' Rainey said, making his voice sound just a little plaintive. 'We was just cuttin' across her land – I mean she's let us do it before – but she's in some sorta woman's tizzy this time, I guess. Started bad-mouthin' us, threatenin' to turn some of her ranch hands loose on us. Bitch even spit in my face, din' she, Murph? Then, suddenly she says we could get outa any real trouble – if she did press trespassin' charges, like – by doin' her a favour.'

'Loretta Munro asked *you* to do *her* a favour?'

'Just as plain as I'm standin' here now, Case. Yeah, well, we din' want no trouble, but she said there'd be no problem if we helped her get some feller who's been roustin' her crew outa her hair. For a consideration, you know?'

McCall said nothing, his face clearly showing he didn't believe a word of what Rainey was saying.

'That feller Buckley's been hasslin' her somethin' awful for some reason she never said....'

'What'd she want you to do?' McCall snapped.

'Aw – well, look, Case, she ... she wanted us to kinda get him off her back – permanent – even if it meant killin' him.'

'Loretta Munro said *that*?'

'We-ell, more kinda *hinted* all round without puttin' it into so many words, but that's what she meant all right, din' she, Murph?'

'Uh? Aw, hell, yeah. We was shocked, Case! I mean a fine-lookin' woman like that offerin' to pay for a killin'...!'

'Wonder what made her choose you two?'

'Aw, don't be like that, Case! We're just—'

'Just lyin' in your teeth, that's what!'

Both hardcases remained silent when they saw the lawman's anger ... and heard it when he cussed them out.

'Never mind the rest of it. Just get the hell outa my sight, and if I hear of anythin' happenin' to Buck Buckley, I'll know right were to come.'

Rainey's eyes were murderous but he looked away quickly. Murphy moaned, grasping his wound, and complained he felt like he was going to faint.

'Well, do it somewheres else, and it better not be in my County. You're still here by sun-up, I'll clap you in jail, get you sent to the chain gang they got workin' on that new road through Hammerhead Swamp. They're expectin' to lose quite a few men when they hit the fever stretch they say. Even asked me to keep it in mind, in case I had any real bad prisoners I wanted to get rid of ... you two could qualify.'

Murphy and Rainey acted as if they weren't quite sure if he was serious or not.

Then the lawman jerked his head. 'Now, git! And don't come back.'

'What about our hosses?' asked Murphy.

'Your problem. Just get outa my County and stay out. If you're thinkin' of sneaking back, well, I can arrange accommodation for you: your address'll be "Care of Boot Hill", though.'

They watched the sheriff ride on up to the crest and over, then looked at each other.

'Hell, I ain't one for walkin', Kel!' Murphy said.

'What you gonna do? Fly? Go back up there an' try to take our broncs away from Craddock? With McCall there to back him? An' we don't even have our guns!'

125

'No, but I was thinkin' – we cut over to Walleye Creek, we can cross on a log ... lots of them there after that big storm a coupla weeks ago—'

'Yeah, yeah, I've seen 'em lyin' all over the place. What the hell's that gonna do for us? It's a goddamn long walk, too!'

'Might be worth it, though. Just beyond that big stand of pines, once we're across, is Craddock's south pasture.'

Rainey frowned, started to make a scathing reply but abruptly stopped, and a slow smile appeared. He clapped Murphy across the shoulder. 'Good thought, Murph! We've got us some hosses.'

Buck was mounted on the chestnut and about to leave the girl when she pointed behind him.

'That looks like the sheriff.'

He hipped in the saddle, recognized McCall riding over the crest. They waited and he told them he had just left Murphy and Rainey.

'Murph had a bullet wound in one arm, claimed you shot him, Buck.' McCall's tone said clearly he wanted some sort of explanation.

'Self-defence – ask her.'

Loretta's mouth tightened at the 'her' but she saw the sheriff looking at her expectantly. Almost reluctantly, she nodded. 'It was ... or near enough, I suppose.'

She didn't look at Buck and he smiled thinly. 'Yeah, near enough'll do, Case.'

'Lemme decide that,' McCall said curtly.

Buck shrugged, waited briefly before McCall said, 'I'll take the word of a lady, I guess.'

'Well, thank you,' Loretta said, a mite uncertainly.

McCall lifted a hand from the saddlehorn. 'Relax, ma'am, I'd take your word any time.'

'That sounds like the Blarney coming out in you, Sheriff!'

'We-ell, I could have a touch of it. All right! Murph and Rainey are gettin' some exercise over the ridge. There anythin' else I should know?'

'No. We only exchanged a few words – nothing serious.'

'You never know with them two, so you ride easy, Buck.' He flicked his gaze to the girl. ' They – hinted – that someone had sort of suggested they might make themselves a little extra cash by putting you outa action.'

'How?' Buck asked, arching eyebrows, watching the girl out of the corners of his eyes.

She was flushing.

'Bushwhack, is my guess,' McCall replied to Buck's question.

'Sounds like someone don't like me much.' He kept looking at the girl but she said nothing – it was obvious she was feeling mighty uncomfortable. Then, when she saw McCall watching her, too, she cleared her throat.

'You mean—' she said, in a voice she barely managed to keep from sounding shaky, 'someone offered money – if they'd kill this man, Sheriff?'

'Ah, just them two lyin' in their teeth again, I'd guess,' Buck said, watching the girl's face but not directly. 'Wouldn't you reckon so, Case?'

'Very likely. But I wouldn't dismiss it altogether – just to be on the safe side.'

After a brief silence, Loretta said, 'I think the sheriff is giving good advice. *Someone* might've offered something....' She was looking at Buck with half-masked defiance and he shrugged again.

'I'll watch my back, then ... just to be on the safe side.'

'Good idea,' Loretta said to Buck. 'If you don't need me, Sheriff...?' she asked tentatively. 'I still have a ranch to run.'

'You like me to escort you home, ma'am?' Buck asked. 'It's on my way – more or less.'

She looked mildly surprised but shook her head.

'No! I'll be all right.'

'I could ride along part way till we reach Walleye Creek...?' suggested Buck, but she gave him a stony look and merely shook her head, turned her mount and galloped off without any farewell.

'You been roustin' her?'

'The hell would I do that for?' Buck looked angry at the lawman's question.

'She ain't usually so touchy.'

'Is that what she is. Makes no nevermind to me.'

'Uh-huh. It's a warm day – an' you owe me a drink, I b'lieve. I recollect right, I paid for the last round.'

'You got a damn good memory!'

'Well, it's a long one. So, how about that drink…? Make it a long one, too.'

'We'll have a big thirst by the time we get to the saloon, so – all right.'

'Mebbe you can buy me two drinks. You owe me one from last Fourth of July.'

Buck shook his head slowly. 'You're right, you've got a long memory, all right – damned long!'

'Aw, just that I've got sore fingers right now.' As Buck looked at him quizzically, McCall said, 'Handlin' money kinda hurts 'em.'

'Hell Almighty! Well, I guess comin' up with a story like that has earned you your damn drinks – OK?'

CHAPTER 11

BURN

The clothes worn by Rainey and Murphy were sodden with dark sweat and torn in a dozen places from staggering through thickly growing bushes when they reached the very southern pasture of Buck Buckley's spread.

Murphy sagged onto a log, breathing hard, sweat streaming down his face. He looked up at Rainey, with a puzzled expression.

'How come you don't sweat as much as me?'

'Dunno, but I do know *my* clothes don't stink like yours do.'

'By hell, Kel! You take some chances!' Murphy gasped, eyes narrowing.

'Aw, I'm safe. You can't match my draw by a long ways.'

Murphy snapped his head up. 'You *tryin'* to push this?'

Rainey glared back, then spread his hands, sinking onto a boulder. 'Nah, nah, forget it, Murph. Just feelin' a mite mean, I guess. I just— Well, look at Craddock's spread – all neat an' tidy, fences all straight, no saggin', his cows carryin' more beef than ours....'

'So—?'

'Aw – jealous, I guess. We bust a gut on that damn hard-scrabble we call a ranch and it looks ... looks abandoned compared to this! We got shingles missin' from the roof, barn's leanin' like a Sat'd'y-night drunk, can count the ribs on our cows, an' our grass is only half as high.'

He kicked at a rock which didn't budge it was set so firmly in the ground. He howled and cussed and danced on one leg, then the other, Murphy laughing out loud.

Rainey started to reach for his gun. ' You think it's funny, huh?'

'Whoa! Whoa, Kel! Sorry, but you – well, I din' know you could dance so good!'

'By Christ! I warned you!'

He went for his gun but Murph was a fraction faster and Rainey stopped with his gun barrel just about to clear leather. His eyes bulged as he let the weapon fall back into the holster and quickly lifted his hands.'

'Easy, Murph! Sorry, pard, you're faster'n you used to be. Just as well Craddock didn't shoot your gun arm, huh? But— Goddammit! I am jealous of this place!'

Slowly, Murphy calmed down and looked around him. 'Yeah, sonuver's got it lookin' good all right.'

Then he grinned. 'Be a shame to spoil it. I mean, if all this nice fresh pasture caught fire an'—' He moistened a fingertip and held it up. 'An' the wind was blowin' towards the house and barn – like now – and so on. Hell! Place'd be a pile of ashes in half an hour.

Murphy blinked, then looked round him slowly.

He turned back to Rainey casually, feeling in his pocket for tobacco sack and papers. 'Feel like a smoke but don't think I've got any vestas....'

Rainey smiled: 'I have! A whole damn fistful!'

Horses were the first priority for a quick getaway after setting the place on fire ... But—

No problem.

They went into the barn, grabbed spare riding gear from the wall pegs, and Rainey took down a plaited rawhide work-rope.

'Aw, now ain't that thoughtful of him,' he said, going out the rear door to the corrals behind the big building, shaking out a noose in the rope.

Several animals were already corralled and it took no time at all to select two – a sorrel for Murphy, and Rainey favoured a big, charcoal-coloured stallion.

'Better grab a gelding,' Murphy advised. 'Way that stallion's hung he'll be chasin' fillies all over the goddamn range and you tryin' to catch him.'

'No he won't, he'll do what *I* want him to.'

Murphy looked doubtful. 'Them big stallions can be a hassle, you know, Kel.'

'I know, but I like him and I'm takin' him.'

'OK, OK – your funeral.'

'Don't sound so goddamn hopeful!'

'Well, *come on*! Let's get started, for Chris'sake.'

Rainey looked at him thoughtfully: it had been a long time since he had heard Murphy sound quite so jumpy.

'Ah, the hell with it,' he murmured, and began bringing out of the vestas he had in his shirt pocket.

Murphy was already piling flammable materials against the wall of the barn: sacking, lengths of wood, a can of pitch, anything that would burn fast. Rainey grabbed a wooden barrow, threw in some straw and old hessian bags, picked up a bottle of turpentine, and wheeled it out into the yard, towards the ranch house.

They delayed a little longer, going through the house for any valuables and didn't hear Buck's two ranch hands come in and cross the front porch: Red Tyler and Sam Hall.

'The hell're you up to, you thievin' sons of bitches!' he shouted.

His companion, Hall, was tall and lanky, in his late forties and balding badly. He held a cocked six-gun and looked mean as a rattler.

'Aw, geez! I nearly pissed myself, you give me such a fright!' said Rainey, spinning around with a shotgun he had taken from a wall rack. He flashed a sickly grin. 'Buck told us to get all the rubbish outa the house. Figurin' on sellin', I think.'

That made the ranch hands blink and Red looked towards the taller one. 'He said nothin' to us....'

Then Murphy stepped into the doorway, spun fast, and his six-gun hammered, followed almost immediately by the thunder of Rainey's shotgun.

The two ranch hands were cut down like a scythe slashing grass. Rainey waved some of the gunsmoke away from his face, coughing twice. 'Judas! I think I mighta pissed myself a little, anyways!'

'Come on, Kel! Get to hell outa here! There could be other hands workin' close by and they'd've heard the shootin'. Come on!'

He was already wrenching the rear door open and leaping down the short set of steps. At the bottom he paused, frowing: Rainey hadn't followed him.

'Kel! Come on, man!'

He heard breaking glass, like someone smashing a whiskey bottle, and then there was a muffled roar and flames shot out of one of the smashed windows. Rainey came stumbling down the steps, slapping at a smouldering shirt sleeve.

'Damn fool! You're goin' without doin' what we came for!' he snarled, then ducked as flames appeared at the doorway where he stood. He jumped down to the ground.

'*Now*, let's get the pasture burnin', then run like hell!'

Buck smelled the smoke as he walked his mount across Walleye Creek and felt his heart lurch.

He'd had a few drinks with McCall and smoked a cigar otherwise he might have smelled the smoke earlier.

Not that it would have made any difference.

Crashing through the clump of trees he saw the front of his house behind a wall of fire. The roof was burning, too, and the pasture was ablaze, the wind blowing the flames towards the house.

He reined down, lifting a hand to protect his face as a blast of heat swept over him. The horse snorted, then whinnied and started to prance uneasily. Buck yanked the reins, turning the mount away, kicking and bullying it in behind the closest clump of trees.

His heart seemed to be pounding up into the back of his aching throat. He screwed up his eyes as swirling smoke stung them. He kept a hand in front of his face, but it was obvious he was too late to do anything to save the house, way too late!

Flames and dark smoke lifted and swirled across the hot blue sky. Once past the line of trees the noise hit him like a thunderclap, had him actually reeling in the saddle as the roof caved in and a wall of heat and gushing sparks had him struggling with the frightened horse again, pulling it around roughly. He didn't have to urge it to race back and stand belly-deep in the creek, big eyes bulging and rolling, nostrils flaring.

He spoke softly to it – didn't even know what he was saying, but that wasn't important: the main thing was to sound as gentle and calm as possible and, together with patting the animal's shoulder, he calmed it down some.

All the while he kept watching his whole damn life

literally go up in smoke … staring with a kind of numbness that engulfed him from boots to hair roots.

Then the others started to arrive.

Neighbouring ranchers would have seen the smoke, of course, and, as was the way of the Frontier, downed tools and came galloping across to see if they could lend a hand. But it was much too late to save anything. All the helpers could really do was sit there out of reach of the roaring flames and watch, secretly thanking the Good Lord that it wasn't *their* place.

Surprisingly, the main conflagration didn't seem to last very long. A huge amount of flames blotted out much of the sky with swirling smoke, roared through the house, then a final burst, and the wall became no higher than a garden fence as there was little left for the flames to feed on.

The fire left nothing but a few blackened uprights smouldering, a couple still with small flames flickering, deformed, shattered windows, their frames glaring like blank eyes.

Sheriff Casey McCall, face blackened and with his clothing burning through in a dozen places like everyone else who had helped fight the blaze, turned to look at the near exhausted Buckley.

'I think some of your herd got clear. Chuck Lorent was drivin' a small bunch over to his place. You know he's only got that smallholding by the bend of the creek, but he said your cows are welcome to stay there till you're ready to bring 'em back.'

'To what?' Buck said bitterly, rubbing his

smoke-reddened eyes with a blistered hand, then gesturing to the smoking ruins, all that was left of his life as a rancher.

'Ah, this is a good valley, Buck, everyone'll pitch in, help you get on your feet again.'

Buck shook his head slowly. 'I dunno, Case, I'm just too bone weary to think straight right now—'

'Hell, man! Shake yourself outa this! You've always been a fighter ... don't let this thing beat you.'

Buck continued to look around him, then spat and raised his raw-looking eyes to the sheriff's face. He nodded briefly. 'Well, whatever I do, I've got nothin' more to lose, that's for sure.'

'That firebreak you made has saved a lot of your graze, that's a good thing – a damn good thing.'

They both glanced up when a rider came up on a nervous horse that had obviously been in the thick of the battle to contain as much of the blaze as possible. It was Loretta Munro, quite dishevelled, face smeared with dirt and smoke.

'We just managed to keep the fire from taking the ridge,' she gasped, gesturing vaguely over one shoulder. 'My men are clearing a little more timber and brush over the far side – just as a precaution. I'll send them up to you here, if you like?'

Casey McCall flicked his gaze to the rancher's dirty face. 'See? You got good neighbours, Buck.'

He nodded, still looking at the girl. 'I-I'd be obliged – much obliged.'

She met and held his gaze. 'No need. Anyone in the

valley would do the same.'

'Mebbe not … anyone,' McCall said, gaining their attention. 'It's obvious this fire was deliberate, so it's not all sweetness and light.'

Buck nodded, face grim. 'I wonder who…?'

'Now hold up, Buck! I'm the law here. I'll look into it and I'll handle it – all the way. OK?'

Buck's face didn't change. 'Whatever you say, Case.'

'Now look! I mean it!'

'All I said was—'

'It was the way you said it! Now, you leave this to me! Or you'll get your fingers burned again – a lot worse than they are now. Savvy?'

Buck looked entirely innocent as he nodded.

'You're the law, Case, I respect that.'

There seemed to be a long, dragging minute of silence, then the sheriff nodded curtly. 'Glad to hear it!'

But he didn't sound quite convinced.

Then a man standing among the charred house ruins, called, 'Sheriff! Got us a coupla bodies here … or what's left of 'em. I think one of 'em might even be still breathin' a little.

CHAPTER 12

RUN THE GAUNTLET

'Goddamn woman!' swore Rainey from behind some trees, high up the ridge overlooking the burned-out ranch. 'If she and her cowhands hadn't jumped in, we'd've taken out his whole damn range, too!'

'What's it matter now?' growled Murphy, sounding quite pleased with himself. 'Just look at Buckley's place. Like a big, big slice of burnt toast – just like that bitch of a wife of mine used to serve me.'

'I never knew you was married.'

'Well, sort of, you know.'

'Where is she now.'

'Hell, I dunno. Came home one time an' she'd gone. Bitch'd sold the damn house – took all the dinero. I got chased off what used to be mine. I'll catch up with her one of these days, though.'

'Geez, you keep things close to your chest.'

Murphy shrugged. 'Never mind that. What d'we do next?'

'Let the sonuver stew over what he's lost for a bit, I guess, then go in an' make his day for him.'

Murphy frowned. 'We gotta watch for that damn McCall though. He'll figure was us burned Buckley out.'

'He'll *think* it was us, but he won't be sure.'

'That won't stop him. Him an' Buckley've always been kinda friendly. They knew each other before Buck came here.'

'Yeah,' Rainey said, slowly nodding his head. 'McCall's a cagey sonuver, tough, too, when he wants to be.'

'But he can't prove nothin'! Hell, we nailed both them ranch hands and the fire musta took care of the bodies. Nah, we ain't got a thing to worry about … just sit back an' watch Buckley fall apart.'

'Christ! He's tougher'n that! He won't just set still, he'll be looking' for whoever done it.'

'You're talkin' like an old woman! There's just nothin' anyone can do to prove was us burned him out.'

'Buckley won't wait for proof, I tell you!'

'Then what's the bettin' McCall'll jump on him with both boots if he tries to nail us? Mac takes his job dead serious. Last votin' time all his handbills said: Vote for Casey McCall – I am the Law! An' he meant it – as we've all found out the hard way. He don't have favourites.'

Rainey was still dubious. Murphy punched him lightly on the upper arm.

'Ah, the hell with it. Let's ride into town, celebrate with a coupla redeyes at the saloon.'

'Yeah. Redeyes – an' red lips.'

'Now you're talkin'!'

'Time to quit talkin' an' do!'

They were almost right.

There were no actual eyewitnesses, so no definite proof could be forthcoming, no matter how strongly they were suspected of causing the fire.

Except ... except for Red Tyler, the short top-hand who worked for Buckley and who had been first through the door of the house when Rainey and Murphy were piling up the most flammable articles.

Red and his companion had both been gunned down mercilessly but Red, when he fell, was partially protected by the old sofa Buck had been repairing in his spare time. It was a mighty solid piece and, when the fire took hold, its weight was too much for the weakened, burning floorboards in that part of the big room, and the sofa crashed through into the small, shadowed space beneath the ranch house.

It took Red Tyler's body with it, and this allowed him to survive the fire, even though he was mortally wounded by Rainey's shotgun blast.

They found his badly burned body when clearing up, mighty surprised that there was still a breath or two of life left in that battered pile of scorched bones and charred flesh.

Red didn't live for long, just long enough to croak the names of the two arsonists he'd surprised in Buckley's house. It took a little while before anyone who heard him whisper the names could decipher them from amongst the grunts and moans, punctuated by Red's screams of pain from his wounds.

Still, in the opinion of those who *had* heard the brave, dying little cowhand, it was unanimous: he'd gasped and choked but named the men who had burned Buckley's house down – with Red and his pard inside – as Rainey and Murphy.

From that moment, those two were dead men, just didn't know it. There were others who would die, too. But the destruction of the ranch house – and the murders of Red Tyler and Sam Hall – would be avenged.

Buck silently swore this and immediately took his firearms and began to clean and tune them all.

Sheriff Casey McCall had been right in his assumption that Buck would hunt down Rainey and Murphy.

No matter what.

Loretta Munro puzzled him.

She had not tried to hide her hatred for him and he had started to worry over just what he could do about it when the fire had wiped him out – or nearly so.

Yet, like many of the folk in the valley, she had sent her own crew in to help, free of any restrictions: they were to do whatever Buck wanted, and the inference was he could call on whatever resources she had, and she would make them readily available.

Buck had led a hard frontier life and he had seen similar things happen before – had, in fact, taken part in several over the years. Now it seemed that it was his turn to be on the receiving end. To quote Casey McCall: *This was a good valley, with good people.*

It bothered his conscience some that he was already planning to take advantage of their generosity.

For the work party, it was essentially a clean-up job, so little could be salvaged from the ruins. It soon became obvious to everyone that Buck Buckley (or Wayne Craddock, whatever you liked to call him) simply didn't belong there. Sure, he was stripped to the waist, sweating, grimy and coughing along with the others, but he just worked, movements mechanical, lifting and straining, throwing, wrenching – whatever it took – like some kind of tireless machine. And all the time three thoughts only were in his head: there was little point in this, nothing could be salvaged for future use; and – the thought uppermost – where the hell were Rainey and Murphy; and, finally, how soon could he get after them! He couldn't just leave all these people here and take off after those killers.

Casey McCall was labouring along with everyone else and he kept looking towards Buck, reading the man's clear impatience in the violent movements he made, blackened face grim as a hangman's.

Eventually, McCall could bear it no longer.

As Buck struggled with a pile of charred timber pinning down the wreckage of the kitchen stove, the sheriff straightened, hands pressing into the small of his back to each the ache for a few moments, before he made his clumsy way through other sweating helpers.

'Buck!' he called, and Buckley rounded almost angrily, glancing up, but not otherwise moving from his work place. The lawman beckoned him with a jerk of his head, pulling out a kerchief and mopping his face.

'What is it, Case?' Buck growled, obviously annoyed at being interrupted in his chore.

'Here!'

For a moment, McCall thought he wasn't going to come, but Buck dropped the corner of the battered stove with a clang and lumbered across.

'What?' he demanded, his impatience and frustration adding a snarl to the single word.

'You're makin' folk nervous.'

'I'm what?'

'You're hurlin' stuff all over the place, not lookin', just throwin' – and hopin' you don't hit anyone. This is pretty damn crowded, man, we don't need any more casualties.'

Buck was frowning, but took time to look around and saw a few helpers staring at him kind of warily.

'Hell! Guess you're right, Case.' He waved, smiling crookedly, raised his raspy voice. 'Sorry, folks! Just tossin' stuff about and imagining it was Rainey or Murphy I had by the throat. Really sorry.'

They waved his apologies away and, as he started to turn back, the sheriff grabbed him by the arm.

'Nice work, Buck. But you don't belong here and—'

'The hell you mean I don't belong here? Judas Priest, where else do I belong? This is all I have left – a pile of goddamn rubble we'd be better off leavin' where it is, 'cause I'll never be able to afford to rebuild.'

'Like I said, you don't belong here. Now, wait up! These folk'll carry on whether you're here or not and I know damn well where you'd rather be.' He paused and looked levelly into Buck's tight face. 'Don't gimme any argument. You're bustin' a gut to get after Rainey and Murphy, ain't you?'

'Well, why the hell wouldn't I be? It's just damn frustrating to be doing this when it's not really accomplishing anything!' He lowered his voice. 'I can't let 'em know that, when they're all givin' me their time and muscles. But, yeah, I'd rather be hunting those—'

McCall whistled softly. 'That's strong language for you! But, all right. Go ahead.'

Buck's frown deepened. 'Go? What the hell're—'

'Get outa here and go find those sons of bitches.'

'Thought you warned me off doin' that?'

'Had to, part of my job to see folk don't take the law into their own hands. But I'm afraid you're gonna explode and scare the hell outa these good folk if you don't do somethin'.'

Buck grinned, starting to move away. 'Obliged, Case! Always knew you had a halfway-human streak in you somewheres!'

'Come back here, you sassy sonuver!' yelled the lawman, dropping a hand to his gun butt.

But he smiled around at the others who had straightened from handling the rubble to see what was happening.

'It's all right, folks. Just carry on doin' a good job. I've sent Buck on a chore. He'll be back soon enough.' He added quietly, 'I hope.'

He didn't explain and the people went back to work, talking among themselves now, throwing strange glances towards him. Buck was already saddling his chestnut in the shade of a few trees that had escaped the main blaze.

Casey McCall hesitated in his own efforts, when saw Buck swing smoothly and quickly into the saddle and get the chestnut moving, tossing the lawman a brief salute.

'Hell. Can't believe I done that!' McCall murmured. 'Givin' him my official OK to go hunt down fugitives.'

Buck couldn't believe it, either, but he wasn't going to worry about the whys and wherefores.

He didn't know exactly where to find Rainey and Murphy, but, like most folk in the County, he knew the general area where the pair hung out. And he knew they would be watching the burned-out ranch – no doubt proud of their handiwork – so he would have to watch where he rode: backshooting wasn't anything that would bother those two.

They, like most of the outlaws or illegal operators in the County, worked out of the hills: there were many places in there to hide fugitives and, occasionally, there were shoot-outs between rival groups, if one trespassed onto land claimed by the others.

In fact, at times, Casey McCall deliberately dropped carefully gathered information about such trespassing where it would do the most good, namely, where the resident group would get to hear of it and go after the intruders.

Some said it was a damned lazy way of keeping the peace, but it worked, though not always, just sufficient times for McCall to make use of the tactic.

He hoped like hell this was one of those times.

Loretta and one of her Mexican ranch hands led the two packhorses across the creek and then rode up through the thin line of trees to the slope beyond. Once there, they gave the horses a rest and she looked around at the line of low hills between her place and Buck Buckley's.

She could see some of the groups of people who had volunteered to help Buck clean up and, while she had been there earlier, she had figured she could do more good by bringing food and drink to the workers.

'Half the town must be there!' she exclaimed aloud, and the Mexican – not far out of his teens – grinned widely, showing brilliantly white teeth.

'*Si*, señorita. He popular, that Señor Buckley. Very quiet, very good. He has helped lot of my people and now it is our turn to do somet'ing for him.'

Loretta nodded curtly. She was doing this chore

147

because she knew it was the right thing to do, but that didn't mean she had changed her opinion of Buck Buckley! She knew nothing could bring back Lew, but—

'Damn you, Buckley!' He had shaken her badly, made her look at her own failure to set Lew on a lawful path. Made her admit – shamefacedly – that Lew might be still alive if she'd had the courage to live up to her role as Big Sister Knows Best, and forced it down the boy's throat. But it was too late now, and— Her teeth tugged at her bottom lip as she fought back rising emotion.

Well, she had never liked Rainey or Murphy, and burning a man out so callously was just the sort of thing they were more than capable of, and they should be made to pay.

If the townsfolk wanted to help Buck then she figured she should too, being the closest neighbour. But she had an uncomfortable feeling that her actions went a little deeper than that and she did not want to think why that might be. So she was surprised to realize she was feeling sorry for him. She did not know him all that well, but knew he was popular, had a name for being generous to folk he figured needed a helping hand and—

'Oh, dammit to hell!' she said aloud, startling the Mexican youth. 'He still killed Lew.'

But she made no move to turn away from the black-ened ruins of Buck's spread.

They were almost to the southern boundary, following the creek, when the Mexican reined down, his eyes big in his narrow, swarthy face, as he called, 'Señorita!'

She looked up sharply, followed his pointing finger and stiffened as she saw two riders coming out of the trees, one on each side, converging on them.

She recognized Rainey and Murphy at once and hauled rein quickly. 'Raoul! Ride back! Ride for the ranch and get Hank Rivers! Tell him to come as fast as he can and to bring at least three men with him! Quickly! Go!'

The youth, more than a little alarmed, whirled his horse and spurred away, lying low behind the startled mount's head.

A rifle whiplashed in two fast shots.

She gave a cry of alarm as the Mexican was lifted from the saddle and crashed to the ground, slim young body spinning and tumbling through the gravel. She felt her gorge rise and quickly looked away from his bloody head and wheeled her own mount.

The rifle crashed again and her horse went down under her. She kicked her feet free of the stirrups and managed to quit the saddle before the mount hit. She struck hard, her body shaken to the core as the ground came up to meet her like a sledgehammer and slammed the breath out of her. Vaguely, head swirling, she heard a man's voice command roughly, 'Get after the kid's bronc, Kel! We'll need it to tie her to when we deliver her to Buckley – *if* we do!'

The words somehow came clearly to her and she

spun towards her dying mount, trying not to watch its face with the rolling eyes begging for help that could never come. As it shuddered in its final throes she reached up and snatched at the rifle butt protruding from the saddle scabbard, which, luckily, was uppermost.

Her hands closed around it as she fell back, her weight pulling the rifle free. Vaguely hearing Murphy shouting something, she forced herself to ignore the buzzing and roaring in her head, levered in a shell and fired in his general direction.

The single shot slapped at her ears and her vision cleared enough to see a startled Murphy suddenly yank his horse aside as lead missed him by bare inches. Rainey was already over the rise, chasing down Raoul's horse and he hipped swiftly in the saddle at the sound of the shot.

'Hey, Murph! Murph!' He started to wheel his mount, but Murphy was already riding towards him, waving wildly.

'Forget the bitch!' he yelled. 'Come on! That was a lucky shot. She ain't got the guts to shoot a man in cold blood!'

But he started abruptly as she clambered to the top of the rise, levering the rifle again. Rainey frowned, started to turn back, but Murphy shouted, 'I said forget her! Buckley's the one we want – come on! Let's go!'

Still Rainey hesitated, but when a bullet burned past his face, he palmed up his six-gun, triggering a wild shot.

She was down on one knee now, the rifle at her shoulder, drawing a careful bead on Murphy. She had him in her sights as he was gesticulating at Rainey, her finger starting to put pressure on the trigger.

Rainey fired at her again but the closeness of her bullet had shaken him and his own aim way way off. Murphy was already riding.

'Come on! We don't need her!'

Still Rainey hesitated and, as her rifle barrel swung to cover him, he muttered, 'Hell with it!' and spurred away.

He crouched low in the saddle and Loretta had his broad back in her sights, finger curled around the trigger, but she couldn't bring herself to shoot.

'Not – not in cold blood,' she murmured. 'I-I can't kill in cold blood.'

She almost wept in frustration, but then lowered the rifle and watched the two men ride out of range.

Shaking, she sat down, cradling the rifle, and her heart skipped a beat at a sound behind her, but it was only Raoul's horse, coming for some company.

She looked at her hands: they were shaking like leaves in a storm.

CHAPTER 13

WIND-UP

Buck rode warily through the narrow cutting McCall had told him about.

'It's just past Weedy Creek, left-hand side going towards MaGill. I've only been there once, but the cutting'll take you through the northern part of the hills. It's actually the lowest section of the range. Best area to cross if you're in a hurry – or don't want everyone and his brother to see you, which is why Rainey and Murphy and others like 'em make use of it. Just hope they're not using it today.'

Buck looked at him steadily. 'You could show me.'

McCall shook his head. 'Outa my jurisdiction – just. That's why it's so popular with the boys who don't much like the law … or me as its representative.'

'Well, wouldn't want *you* to break any laws, I guess—'

'Not me. I'm just here to help.'

Buck smiled wryly. 'Help – who?'

McCall spread his arms. 'Whoever asks. Hey! Now I come to think of it, you never asked, did you?'

'Only where was the best place to find Rainey and Murphy.'

'I shouldn'ta mentioned it. Guess I must like you, Buck.'

'When you want me to do your job for you!'

'Now that ain't fair. I don't know for sure if Rainey and Murphy burned your ranch down. I mean, they'd do it, all right, but where's your proof?'

Buck tapped his forehead and the sheriff smiled.

'Yeah, but won't stand up in court. Still, if you was to bring in those men and they confessed—' He stopped suddenly, frowning. 'Mind, I doubt they'd do it voluntarily and it'd be kinda rough puttin' 'em in the right mood, but such things can be arranged.' He paused, then added, 'So I hear.'

Buck shook his head slowly. 'You're a damn hypocrite, McCall! The way you go on about someone getting under your neck or trying to get around the law and yet you'll do it yourself.'

Very sober now, McCall said: 'My privilege. I'll do whatever it takes to nail anyone I *know* is breaking the law.'

'Including using someone like me to flush a couple of arsonists for you.'

The sheriff's deadpan expression didn't change. 'Whatever it takes. Or, mebbe you can add *whoever* it takes ... long as the job gets done, preferably by someone who has a vested interest in seein' the best results.'

Buck nodded slowly. 'All right. Can I depend on back up from you if I need it?'

'What kind of back up you mean?'

'Could be your guns.'

'That's one of them things I'd have to decide when the time came. You got proof – an' I mean real proof that'll stand up in court?'

'There's Red Tyler's dying words …'

'Make a good newspaper story, but it'd depend on the judge whether he accepted it or not. Look, I'm gettin' older, and I aim to collect *all* of my retirement pay. I'm at the point where I aim to dot all my 'I's' and cross all by 'T's' so there's nothin' to stop me gettin' what's my due. That's why I don't want anyone – *anyone* – goin' in in a blaze of glory, messin' things up, and then say they was actin' on my behalf – or information I give 'em. See what I'm gettin' at?'

'Sure. Like I said: you're a damn hypocrite!'

McCall's face tightened. 'I'll let you have that one, but that's all. Nothin' more. Now, you wanta go after Rainey and Murphy. OK, do it. I'm givin' you the chance. Do what you figure you have to, anythin' that makes you feel better. But if it goes wrong—' He shrugged. 'Remember, I did warn you not to rush into things without reliable proof: *reliable* proof that'll stand up in court.'

Buck looked disgusted. 'I'll make sure your ass is covered, McCall!'

'Enough! I got my own life to look out for and that's what I aim to do. Now, if you wanta go find those fellers you suspect've done you wrong, be my guest.'

'Well, I need some fresh air anyway. *Adios.*'

'Feel free to call on me if you need a hand.'

Buck paused, then just waved and moved off, shaking his head slowly. *That damn McCall!*

He should have realized those two, Rainey and Murphy, would be ready for any move he made against them. But he would have been surprised to know they didn't really blame him for gunning for them.

'Hell, I'd be riled, too, someone put a torch to my house,' Murphy had said, and Rainey nodded slowly.

'But we can't stand still for anythin' like that, Murph. We *get* him – see him planted on Boot Hill before we quit this place.'

'Wouldn't've minded takin' that gal along,' mused Murphy. 'Pity she got away.'

'Yeah, but too much damn trouble travellin' with *any* woman, I reckon. Forget her and concentrate on them fifty thousand pesos. Make a better picture, don't they?'

Murphy looked disappointed at first, but then nodded enthusiastically. 'OK. Let's go get the sonuver!'

Buck had stayed under cover and watched Rainey and Murphy approaching what was left of his spread.

He was hiding in the tumbledown remains of one of the toolsheds, in fact, the only ranch building with enough plank wall still standing to hide him, though it was badly charred. The only trouble was, there was a wide gap between a couple of the warped planks and while he tried to keep away from them, he stumbled and fell against them, right over the crack, and his almost new, bright blue shirt flashed in the sun for a fraction of a second.

It was enough for Murphy to spot, just turning so his back was to the wind to shield the match he was using to light his cigarette. He swore when the wind blew out the flame just as the bright shirt showed like a beacon at the gap ... a flash. Like blue lightning catching his eye.

'Holeee Joe!' he breathed. 'Kel. Kel!' His voice now only a harsh whisper alerted Rainey to the fact that there was someone close by who might hear.

Rainey moved like a ghost and was beside his pard in three long strides. Murphy pointed to the plank: and the warped section where Buck's shirt was still showing – not too much now the direct sunlight had moved a few inches, but enough to be seen against the charred wood.

Guns in hands, they exchanged a deadly glance, but one loaded with satisfaction.

Rainey nodded and made signs with his hands towards the charred wall of the old toolshed. They had worked in unison for long years and the sign language was minimal but more than adequate.

Rainey went left, Murphy to the right. Together they dropped to their knees, brought up their guns and began firing.

The Colts bucked and roared and spat flame and smoke. The lead tore up the plank in a shower of splinters as they stood slowly, instinctively reloading even as they waited for the smoke to clear so they could see their handiwork properly.

Then Buck Buckley stepped into view, apparently from *behind* the old shed's remains, his gun bucking, spitting fire and lead.

Murphy went down first. He'd opened his mouth to cry a warning to Rainey, but one slug closed that mouth forever or, rather, opened a permanent new hole in his face. As blood sprayed and teeth splintered, Murphy, lifted off his feet by the lead's impact, crashed in a crumpled heap, landing almost against Rainey's legs.

The big man leapt out of the way, started to run towards the trees, skidded and spun around, dropping swiftly to his knees. And that was how he died, kneeling, trying to fan his gun at the crouching Buck.

The gun in Buck's fist rose slightly as he triggered his last two shots. They caught Rainey just beneath the throat and he went down in a violent, twisting half-somersault, his body landing across one of the dead Murphy's outstretched legs.

Buck leaned against the shaky wall and reloaded.

When he had examined the dead men – making sure they were dead – he stood and looked back at the charred wall. From this angle, it looked as if that end of the original shed was still standing, giving the impression that the shed itself was mostly whole, enclosed, but badly burned.

But the angle of observation changed dramatically when he moved a few feet to the left: it showed that there *was* the charred wall all right, and one other, at right-angles, but that was all. Even though they looked as if they enclosed part of the entire shed, they did not actually meet. No doubt this was why Rainey and Murphy had been so surprised when Buck stepped out and cut them down. They had thought he was inside a roofless shed … trapped.

Buck had the two bodies wrapped in blankets and some old sacks when people came riding in to see what all the shooting was about.

McCall listened to Buck's explanation, stuck a cheroot between his teeth and fired up.

'See your wall's got holes in it like a damn sieve. No wonder it sounded like the Battle at Bull Run.'

'Dunno, wasn't there.'

'Damn smart-mouth Reb! Hey! Where you goin'?'

'Home.' He pointed. 'Just up the slope there.'

'Gonna be a while before you can call *that* home.'

'Mebbe, but I've got the time to fix it up.'

'You're stayin' then?'

Buck looked at him steadily. 'Where would I go?'

McCall's eyes pinched down a little. 'Well, the land's yours, or what's left of it.'

'Like I said, I got the time to rebuild. No money, but I'll sign on with a few trail herds. I'll fix it up decent eventually … on a smaller scale, but I'll get there.'

'I believe you will, you stubborn son-of-a-bitch.' McCall inclined his head slightly. 'Hope you do,' he added, then stuck out his right hand. 'Good luck.'

'Yeah,' said Buck, as he gripped with the lawman. 'Reckon I've had my share of the other kind.'

'Uh-huh.' The sheriff was looking past Buck and he gestured briefly. As Buck turned, curiously, he saw Loretta coming towards them, a little dishevelled and looking weary, a rifle resting across one shoulder.

'Mebbe you're due for a change of luck, all right,' McCall said quietly. 'Have to put in a little work, I guess, but probably be worth it.'

'You reckon...?'

'Only one way to find out.' McCall started to turn away, then paused. 'By the way, think your luck's already started to change.'

Frowning, Buck waited, one eye on the approaching girl.

The sheriff snorted. 'Doc Gordon told me a while back that he was called out to *El Capitano*'s. The man's mighty poorly and, accordin' to Doc, headin' for a mighty big heart attack.'

Buck stiffened. 'How come?'

'That Spanish temperament – got him all worked up. And the word is his wife is just waiting for him to die and then she's goin' back to Spain. Seems she never wanted to come here in the first place. You know what that means, don't you?'

'Not really game to think about it.'

'Well, reckon it'll make pleasant thinking. Means no

more bounty. She'll take every cent with her. Go back to her own family and, I s'pose, marry some Don – and forget all about her time here.'

'And you just remembered to tell me this?'

McCall shrugged. 'Memory's not what it used to be. You'll find out as you get older.'

Buck smiled as Loretta came up, a little breathless from the climb. 'Long as I've got things I want to remember.'

The girl looked at him, puzzled, and McCall managed a crooked smile.

'I'd say your chances are pretty good. Need a little time, mebbe, but— Nice to have good neighbours, eh?'

The girl frowned. 'What're you two grinning about?'